Lance

Hathaway House, Book 12

Dale Mayer

Books in This Series:

Aaron, Book 1

Brock, Book 2

Cole, Book 3

Denton, Book 4

Elliot, Book 5

Finn, Book 6

Gregory, Book 7

Heath, Book 8

Iain, Book 9

Jaden, Book 10

Keith, Book 11

Lance, Book 12

Melissa, Book 13

LANCE: HATHAWAY HOUSE, BOOK 12
Dale Mayer
Valley Publishing Ltd.

Copyright © 2020

ISBN-13: 978-1-773363-84-4
Print Edition

About This Book

Welcome to Hathaway House. Rehab Center. Safe Haven. Second chance at life and love.

Lance Mayfair sought out Hathaway House at the recommendation of a friend, who told him it was an answer to prayer. Lance knows more about prayers than answers, but, if he can see progress in one particular area of his life and health, it will be worth the effort and the pain. He'll do anything he can to play music again. It's all he has left now that his days as a Navy SEAL are over and, with them, any chance of a happy, productive life.

However, the shoulder injury that ended his career pretty much guarantees he'll never play his beloved instruments ever again.

Unless Hathaway House and Jessica can work a miracle.

Jessica has worked with many patients at Hathaway House, but she connects with Lance in a way she didn't with any of the others. She can see the need inside him—his desire to create again, to heal through music. And his goal becomes her goal: to see him play music in his soul again.

Only his music isn't all he wants or needs, and making him happy goes a long way to making her happy, but it's not enough. Both want and need so much more.

Prologue

LANCE MAYFAIR STARED at the picture from Iain. In fact, multiple photos. None of them were registering as being from his friend. How was that even possible? Iain had left the same VA hospital where Lance still was, but Iain had been a mess. A determined jokester but somebody who would turn his life around. They hadn't talked too long or too deep about their real issues because it had been painful for them all. But Lance never really expected to hear from Iain again. Instead, here he was, sending photos and letting Lance know that there was life after the VA hospital. Not only life but a crazy-good life. Lance stared in shock, and then he read the message again.

The text message with the photos was simple. **Get here. It'll make all the difference in the world.**

Lance quickly responded and wrote, **But will it? Or is it just more false hope?**

Iain answered almost immediately. **No, it's not false hope at all.**

And then his phone rang. Lance picked up and answered, knowing it would be Iain. "Are you sure? Because, man, these look like they've been through Photoshop. Many times over."

Iain's laughter boomed through the phone. "I know they do," he said. "However, I would never steer you wrong. It's a

1

completely different world now. Take a look at that last photo. That is me right now," he said. "So compare that to where I was when you saw me last."

"It's unbelievable," he said.

"I know it's unbelievable, but it happened here, and you can do it too. Don't mess up. This is one of the biggest opportunities you'll ever have," he said. "Send in your application, and I'll put in a good word."

And, with that, Iain hung up and left Lance to his rather dark thoughts. It was hard to be in the same place forever with no progress. The doctors had pretty well decided he was as good as he would get, and that was it. So what would he do with his life? How was he supposed to deal with that when everything seemed to be so off-kilter? It's not what he wanted for his life. This wasn't what he expected, and so much anger was inside that he just didn't know how to deal with it.

If he listened to Iain, Lance might have another chance at something more, but that didn't mean that Iain's progress would be the progress Lance would see. And that was one of the hardest things he had experienced in life. Realizing that something worked for everybody else, but you were the one exception. You were the guy it wouldn't work for. He didn't want that. He didn't want any more of that same depressing "likely to be your future" results.

But, after looking at those photos, Lance wondered about that small voice which asked Lance if he really would pass up the one opportunity that might make a difference. And, of course, he didn't dare. Because his world hinged on it. He quickly followed the link in the email to the Hathaway House application form. He looked at it, took a slow but deep breath, and quickly downloaded the file.

If he just filled it out and sent it in, that action alone was a whole different story. He could at least say he tried. With one last look at the photos from Iain, Lance completed the application, quickly attached it to an email, and sent it off, using Iain's and Jaden's names as references. Because Lance would do anything he could to be that man who Iain had showed him was possible.

Now Lance just had to hope that one more miracle was left for him too.

Chapter 1

LANCE'S ARRIVAL SEEMED to be just one more blip in the long day, both his stamina and his patience put to the test as he waited at Hathaway House to be admitted. The chaos at the front reception desk did little to ease his own insecurity about his arrival here or his confidence in his decision. In the back of his mind he couldn't help but remember that Iain was a joker of the highest order. What if he had been joking with all those emails back and forth, with the photos that had inspired a little flicker of hope in Lance's seemingly hopeless situation?

Again he thought, *Those pictures could have been easily altered by Photoshop.* They could have been doctored enough to make it look like Iain was something he wasn't anymore. Although that would have been a joke gone too far. Lance had even asked him outright, and Iain had tried to alleviate his fears, but it was hard. Miraculously Lance's application had been accepted, and he was now committing to a massive change in his world, and it was all because of Iain. Lance knew Jaden was here too, and maybe that was a good thing.

Lance currently sat in a wheelchair, shaky from the long trip, parked off to the side of the reception area, a big man, an orderly, holding on to Lance's chair.

Just then a whistle broke through, and a small woman stepped from her office off to the side, and, with a glare, said,

"What is going on here?" The receptionist looked relieved as she stepped forward.

"Dani, we have a problem. Steven here is trying to leave, and Jonathan is here to check in. But Steven isn't supposed to go until tomorrow, at least according to my records. Jonathan says he was supposed to be in today, but I'm not seeing it."

Dani shook her head. "So, they're assigned to the same room. Is that the idea?"

The receptionist nodded, blowing a strand of hair from her flushed face.

Dani looked at Steven and said, "Steven, we went over this. Today is Tuesday. Your bride is coming Wednesday."

He frowned at her. "No, see? They told me Tuesday," and he held up a cell phone.

She looked at the cell phone message. "Well, that may be, but you haven't been signed out of here yet. The doctor only approved you to leave tomorrow. So, if you make changes to your arrangements," she said, "you have to let us know."

He looked at her, looked at his phone again, and said, "Oh. But this guy wants in today, so why can't I just leave early?"

"I'm not saying you can't," she said, "but I have to get the doctor to sign off on this." She turned to look at the new arrival. "And you must be Jonathan, correct?" She reached out a hand. He nodded and shook her hand. He was at least ambulatory from what Lance could see. She smiled and said, "So you're a day early. How come?"

Jonathan shrugged and said, "I was supposed to spend the night in town, but the hotel didn't have a room for me for some reason, so I took a shot and had a cab bring me straight here."

"Figuring that we might have a room for you instead?" she said with a note of humor.

He had the grace to look ashamed. "I know I'm not expected until tomorrow."

"No, you aren't," she said. "However, it's not the end of the world. So why don't you both go sit down and give us a chance to sort this out." Then she turned and looked at Lance. She took several steps over, held out her hand, and said, "So, you're a new arrival as well, right?"

"Yes, ma'am. I'm Lance," he said.

"Good," she said. "You, I was expecting." A note of humor was in her voice, and he was amazed that she had kept her cool as much as she could.

She said, "I'm Dani, and I run this place with my father," she said, as she turned to the receptionist and said, "Melanie, Lance's room should be ready."

The receptionist quickly made several clicking motions on the keys, then looked up and nodded. "Yes, he's in room 1214."

"Good," Dani said. Turning back to Lance, she smiled, motioned at the big man standing behind Lance, and said, "I'll let Jim here take you to your room. I'll be there in a few minutes with your introduction package, and we'll go over everything you need to know. Is that okay?"

He nodded and smiled. "Of course. I'm assuming you'll get this fixed first," he said with a wave to the other two guys.

"Let's hope," she said, stepping out of the way with a smile. Jim, the big burly orderly behind Lance, immediately picked up Lance's bags, tossed them over his shoulders, and pushed his wheelchair out and away from the reception area.

"Well, I'm glad I have a proper room at least," he said.

Jim laughed. "It happens," he said. "At every center everybody always wants to leave early, and we do get a few people who try to come in early, but it does mess up the count on the available beds. We're always full up, so it's not like we can just shuffle out a bed for an unexpected visitor."

He wondered at that. "I guess there's also all the cleaning and housekeeping that has to be done when a room changes over."

"Top to bottom," Jim said, a smile in his voice. He pushed Lance down a long hallway, with several short hallways leading off to the sides. They passed a large open game room, where several guys were playing pool, others reading, and a big screen TV played with a basketball game on.

"So, what's this? A common room?"

"One of them," he said, sounding cheerful as they passed another hallway.

From that area Lance heard the sounds of dishes clinking together. "So, somewhere down there is the cafeteria?"

"Exactly," he said. "Once we get you settled in your room," he said, "and depending on how you feel, I can either grab you a cup of coffee or whatever you want or maybe take you around for a little bit of a tour until Dani comes."

"Not a bad idea, at that," he said. "Any idea if Jaden is still here?"

"Jaden, Jaden, Jaden," he muttered. "*Hmm*, I'm not sure I remember that one," he said. "It's a big place though, and we're generally assigned to one area, so we all get to know each other better in our own sections."

"That's okay," he said. "I'll find out soon enough."

"Friend of yours?"

"Yeah," he said. "I was just hoping maybe I could see him before he leaves."

"If he's here, you sure will," he said. "First things first, so let's get you into your room."

They kept moving down the hallway, and then he turned a corner and then another corner. "Wow, you're right. This is a big place."

"You have no idea," he said. As they came to the end of the hallway, on the right-hand side was an open door. Jim wheeled him in and said, "This is your room. Got your own bathroom, and you look out over the horses," he said. "Hopefully that's not a hardship for you."

"I still struggle with the fact that you have animals right here with you," he said.

"Yeah, I know, but that's one of the joys of the place."

"I agree," he said. "It's pretty special."

With Jim's help, Lance made the couple steps from the wheelchair to the bed. When he sank down onto the bed, he shifted his weight backward and stretched out and groaned with relief.

"How about I help you raise the head of the bed a little bit," he said, "and I'll show you how the mechanics work." Together they adjusted the bed so Lance was at a better angle and much more comfortable.

From there, he could even look out over the horses and the pastures. His gaze was drawn to the green grass, the white fences, and the animals free to move about. "It's a beautiful view," he said.

"It is. Almost everybody on this side gets a similar view," Jim said. He dropped Lance's bags over by a wall with built-in cupboards and said, "When you get rested up a bit and feeling better, you can unpack over here. If you need help, just let somebody know, and one of us will give you a hand."

He nodded. "That sounds great," he said. "It's been a very long day."

"That's why I would offer you a cup of coffee or some water," he said. "Something to hold you over until Dani gets here."

"Do you think she'll be all that long?"

"Nope," Jim said. "Dani is really good at sorting out stuff like that."

"Glad to hear it," he said, laughing. "I don't envy her that job."

"It's her place," Jim said, "so, for her, it's less about a job and more about a passion."

"Oh, that's right," he said. "I did hear something about that."

"She started the place for her father, and, once she got it going, a tsunami of others with like needs came here too," Jim said, his tone respectful.

"That's cool," Lance said, feeling hopeful.

Jim headed for the door and said, "Coffee? Or something else?"

Lance leaned back, thought about it, and said, "How about a hot cup of tea instead?"

"You got it," he said. "Milk? Sugar?"

"A little bit of milk would be great, thanks." And, just like that, Jim left. Lance should get up and unpack. It was part of his motto for life to do what he needed to do today and to not push it off, but his body was just too sore and too tired to tackle it now. He thought, if he could curl up under a blanket, he'd sleep. But he lay on top of the blankets, and it was way too much of a headache to try to get under them. Besides, he didn't want to be asleep when Dani arrived. He still had yet to be properly introduced to the place. He was sure he had a mess of paperwork to handle as well. Jim came back with the tea, just a few minutes later.

"Here you go. If you need anything else, you've got a buzzer right beside you," he said. "Seriously, don't hesitate if you need it for anything. Somebody will come to your aid." And, with that, he took off.

Lance leaned back and sipped his tea, but, when he heard light footsteps coming down the hallway, he wasn't surprised to see Dani walk in with a bright smile on her face. "Did you get the rooms all sorted out?"

"All sorted," she said. "There aren't all that many places like this where people are so eager to get into it, right?" she said with a laugh.

He smiled. "Well, it's good advertisement if nothing else."

She nodded. "And how are you doing after your trip?"

"Questioning my choice," he said bluntly. "Double questioning actually."

"I get it," she said. "So, double question all you want, but you're here, so make the best of it. An awful lot of good work is happening in Hathaway House."

"I hope so," he said, shifting in the bed.

"You look worn out," she said. "Do you want to catch a nap before dinner?"

"I was thinking about it," he said, "but I'm lying on the blankets, and that seems like way too much trouble to deal with."

She walked over to the cupboard, pulled out another blanket, and, opening it up, she spread it across him. "More linens and such are always in the cupboard, and, if you find that you need something that's not there, just let us know."

Then she said, "Now I have a packet for you." She proceeded to go over the details on his own personal iPad, showing him how it worked. She went over his team, listing all the people who would come by to see him. Then she went to a general information tab, where information about meals could be found and about how the system here works. "Dinner will start in forty-five minutes, so, if you want to have a rest, go for it. You've got a two-hour window for eating dinner from the buffet line," she said, "but, if you happen to sleep through a meal and wake up afterward, not to worry. Just go on to the cafeteria. There will always be food for you," she said.

He nodded. "That's good to hear." He hesitated and then said, "I know Iain."

"Yes. Iain recommended that you come here," she said. "I also heard you know Jaden."

"Yeah." He hesitated. "Is Jaden still here?"

"He is, indeed," she said. "He'll be here for another month or two, and Iain comes back and forth. By the way, he's partnered up with one of our vet techs down below, so the two of them are here on a regular basis."

"Good," he said. "I'd like to see him."

"Just making sure the pictures he's sending out aren't altered by Photoshop?" she teased, with a big grin.

He took a deep breath and said, "Is that so wrong of me?"

"No, not at all," she said, some of her laughter slipping away. "It's normal," she added. "You need to see the proof, and Iain is definitely walking proof."

"It just seems so unbelievable," he said. "Plus the guy I knew was this jokester."

"Well, he presented that facade to everybody," she said.

12

"He's a very different person now. He helps out on various carpentry jobs for the vet clinic."

"That sounds like him. He always did have a dabbler's hand at fixing things."

"I'll let him know you've arrived, if you like. And I'm on my way around, talking to a few other people, so I'll stop in at Jaden's and tell him that you're here too."

At that, Lance smiled. "I'd really appreciate it. Kind of makes the arrival less ..." He let his voice trail off.

"It's always nice to see a friendly face," she said firmly. "But, before long, this place will be home to you anyway."

He nodded and smiled. "If you say so."

"I do," she said with a laugh. "So, your intake nurse will be in soon. She'll come in to check your blood pressure and to make sure the trip was not too arduous. She'll go over your current medications and update your file. Her name is Jessica, so say hello and be nice because you'll be seeing quite a bit of her, especially at first."

"Sounds good," he said, and, with that, Dani disappeared. On the heels of that visit, a woman with a shock of red hair stepped inside. She had freckles across both cheeks, and her eyes were bright green. He was mesmerized. "Wow," he said, "that might be the reddest hair I've ever seen."

"Thank you. I think," she said in a bright voice.

"No—I only meant—" Flustered, he continued, "Well, I like it."

She giggled. "One can never tell. Some people like it. Others think I am cursed. As for me, it is what it is at this point." Laughing, she walked over and said, "Hi, I'm Jessica. Let's have a look at you."

13

JESSICA MARLOW LOVED the teasing and the way that he interacted with her. She knew it was meant to distract from his pain, and, while he'd be the first to deny it, clearly the trip had been a lot for him. She quickly slipped the blood pressure cuff over his arm, pumped it up, and checked his reading. Frowning that it was high but not excessively so, she checked his temperature and then his pulse. When she was done, she went over his medications, bringing up the chart on her tablet so he could see them. Together, they confirmed everything. Then she went on.

"Now I'm sure Dani explained that everybody on your team will be coming in and out most of today because you're a new arrival, and then, if anybody wants any testing done, that'll start tomorrow."

"Great. So I get to be a pincushion again." He groaned.

"Sorry, it's a stage of life."

"Does that stage ever come to an end though?"

"It does," she said. "I'm sort of new here myself, compared to some of the others. I've been here for ten months. I've seen several people leave in great shape."

"Yeah, but were they in bad shape when they arrived? That is the real question."

"Good point," she said. "Have faith." She nodded, giving him a perky smile. "I know everything will work out."

"I do have faith," he said, "otherwise I wouldn't be here at all."

"Tough trip?"

"Tougher than I expected," he admitted.

She moved around his room with efficient movement. She didn't make any extra steps or repeat any movements. She knew what she was doing. "You know what? I have a few extra minutes. Do you want me to help you unpack?"

"I can do it tomorrow," he said, not wanting to impose on her.

She looked at him with one eyebrow raised and said, "Right now you have somebody here who's available to help. If you're the kind of person who doesn't feel like he's actually settled in until he's unpacked, let's take care of it right now."

"Would you mind?" he said. "I'm not used to having other people do things for me."

"In this place," she said, "we all do for everybody, and there isn't anybody who doesn't get help when they need it." At that, she quickly opened his duffel bag, organized the clothing, and put them away in drawers. "I'm glad to see you brought swim shorts," she said. "The pool is a major part of your program here."

"Pool?"

She turned in surprise. "I thought you knew."

"You'd think I would know," he said, "because I'm friends with a couple guys who have been here or still are, but I don't think anybody mentioned the pool."

"When we get around to giving you a full tour," she said, "you'll see. Make sure you talk to your physiotherapists about our water program, if you like. Otherwise they often wait a few weeks, if not longer, before letting people into the pool."

"Don't worry," he said. "Now that you've mentioned it, I'll be right on his case."

"Good," she said. Once everything was put away, she folded up the duffel and tucked it in the bottom of the closet.

"Now," she said, "is there anything else I can do for you?"

He immediately shook his head.

"What about dinner?" she asked, giving him a straight-forward look. "Are you strong enough to get down there for dinner tonight?" She motioned at the wheelchair. "I saw you arrive and noticed Jim pushing you down the hallway. I can certainly take you to dinner, if you're ready."

He hated to even ask and shook his head, embarrassed.

"Remember," she said. "There are no *shoulda, coulda, wouldas* at this place," she said. "You're either strong enough to make your way down there on your own—and I'll show you where it is—or I'll take you there."

He stared at her wordlessly and collapsed against the bed. "I haven't eaten all day," he said, "so I should, but honestly, it seems like it's an awfully long way to go."

Frowning, she said, "It's your first day, so, if you'd like me to pick up something, I can do that too."

He really liked that option, but the thought of asking her to do even more went against the grain.

"The other option is," she said, "I can take you down there, you can pick out something, and we can bring it back here for you."

"Well, that's a compromise," he said. "Maybe that one?"

"Done," she said. She brought the wheelchair to the head of the bed and then moved something forward from under the bed. A set of steps for him. "I presume you'll need these for a few days."

With a wince, he said, "Yeah, I think so." He straight-ened up, gasping, as he worked muscles that hadn't worked in a very long time. She immediately stepped up, moved the wheelchair into a better position, then reached out for his arm. He didn't even think about it before grabbing hers for support. Very slowly, like a crippled old man, he made his way down the steps and into the wheelchair. He shook in place for a moment, while she grabbed the blanket and wrapped it around his legs.

"Come on. Let's go pick you up some dinner. We'll get you some hot tea, since yours is gone already. Then we'll get you back to bed."

He didn't argue, since he knew he needed to eat. Left to his own devices, his stomach would set off a chain reaction that would keep him awake all night if he didn't get a chance to eat. But, at the same time, it was hard and went against the grain to let other people do things for him. He'd been doing so much better at the last place, and now it's like he'd taken a complete step back.

"I wouldn't worry about it," she said. "This is temporary."

He twisted ever-so-slightly. "What is temporary?"

"When most people arrive, they find that they're set back a bit from their travels. They always assume it'll be a quick and easy adjustment, but it's actually worse than anything."

"If you say so."

"I do," she said with a laugh.

He vaguely recognized some of the trip back to where he thought the cafeteria was.

"It's a little bit early, so that's good. Still the rush will be coming soon enough though." At that, she pushed him forward and stopped at the edge of the counter, grabbing a tray for him. She placed it on his lap and said, "Okay, we can carry it back that way." Then she picked it up and put it back on the counter and pushed it and him along the front of the buffet line, where a huge male oversaw the food. "Dennis, we have a new arrival."

Dennis poked his head over the top, then grinned and

said, "Hi, I'm Dennis. The kitchen is mine. What can I get you?"

Lance hated the shakiness he felt inside and said in the heartiest voice he could muster, "Something hot that will go down easy."

"Well, I've got fish stew, fried chicken, and some skewers of meat and veggies here."

"How about the stew?" he said. "Maybe with a slab of bread on the side."

"You got it," he said. "How big of a bowl do you want?"

Immediately Lance shook his head. "Not too much," he said. "I haven't eaten all day, and my stomach will revolt as it is." At that, Dennis frowned but served up a medium-size bowl, added a couple thick slabs of French bread buttered on the side, and asked, "How about some food for your room? You want to take a muffin or a sandwich back, in case you need more later?"

"I don't really want to," he said, and then he started to shiver. Jessica immediately checked his temperature. "Let's get you headed back to bed," she said. "Dennis, maybe send somebody to check on him in a couple hours, just to make sure he doesn't need more to eat? We'll get this hot food down. I'll just pick him up some hot tea and get him back to bed."

Dennis watched them with a frown on his face.

She gave him a reassuring smile and said, "He should be fine, once he gets rested up."

"I'm counting on you to make sure he is," Dennis said. "I haven't lost one yet."

She chuckled at that. "It's okay, Lance. We're heading back to your room now," she said. "I'm sorry. I hadn't realized you were feeling that bad."

"I don't know if it's that bad or not," he said. "All of a sudden I just felt pretty shaky." They were back in his room within minutes. He looked at his bed with relief, as she picked up the tray, put it on a small table, backed the wheelchair up, and put down the locks to help him to his feet.

"Bathroom first?"

He groaned and said, "Yeah."

She walked over and asked, "Can you use crutches?"

"Yeah, I can probably make those few steps," he said, and, using the crutches, she watched as he made his way to the bathroom. When the door closed, she stood and waited.

It took a few minutes for him to come back out. Sweat was on his forehead, and he looked even worse. She immediately walked over, gave him a shoulder for support, then helped him into bed. "Do you have pajamas?"

"Yeah, we put them away," he gasped out.

She came back with a folded pair of blue checked pajamas, and, before he realized it, she already had his shirt off, the pajama top on, his socks and jeans off, and had him into the pajama bottoms. Before he could even say anything, she had him tucked under and relaxed in the bed with the blanket up around him. She quickly folded up his clothes and put them in the laundry bin, then moved the table over. "There. How's the angle for eating?"

"I need to be a little straighter," he said.

She handed him a remote. "Try this."

Ever-so-slowly, he managed to get it to work. He sighed. "I'm so tired," he said, "but I need food." He picked up a spoon, took a bite, and then sank back against the bed. "Wow," he said. "This is really good."

"It is," she said, "and you need to take full advantage of

it. I'll go get you some hot tea and some water and will be right back." With that, she bolted again to the kitchen. She didn't want him to know how worried she was about him. She hadn't seen anybody arrive with the shakes like that. As soon as she got him some drinks, she would talk to the doctor and make sure somebody came and checked up on him tonight.

Dennis saw her as she came back in. "Is he okay?"

She shook her head. "Exhausted, shaky, and maybe in a little bit of shock," she said. "I'm not exactly sure what's going on, but I'll mention it to his doctor." She picked up tea and a bottle of water and a bottle of juice. "I'm not sure if he has any blood sugar issues either," she says, "but I'll take him a juice just in case." She flashed Dennis a smile and sped back out again and headed for Lance's room. When she got there, his bowl of stew was almost empty, and he had some color in his face. She put the drinks down for him. "You're looking better already."

"Yeah, I think it was just the whole travel-and-arrival thing," he said, leaning back. "I really want another bowl of stew, but I don't think I can get any more down."

"How about another bowl in an hour or so?"

"How does that work?" he said with a laugh. "I'm sure they have better things to do than cater to me."

"Look. Like I said earlier, I haven't been here that long myself, but one thing was made very clear to me when I started work here," she said with quiet emphasis. "Nobody has anything better to do than to look after you and the other patients here. Obviously taking you down there and back wasn't the best decision. I should have realized how tired you were and should have just gone and collected you some food."

"But you probably wouldn't have chosen stew for me," he said, a smile at the corner of his lips. He looked down at the empty bowl and said, "I think I would like a second bowl. But I feel guilty."

"Don't," she said, as she snagged up the bowl. "I brought you tea, juice, and water. Is there anything else you would like?"

He shook his head. "Maybe just seconds on stew." There was such a hopeful look on his face that she had to laugh.

"I don't have a problem doing that," she said. "So hang on. I'll be right back." She headed down the hallway with the empty dish. When she walked back into the cafeteria, she showed it to Dennis, and a big smile broke out across his face.

"Now that I like to see," he said.

"Even better," she said, "please, sir, he'd like some more."

He chuckled at the Oliver Twist reference and took the dirty bowl from her and filled up a clean one. "Here. Take this one to him."

Rather than carry it on a tray, she grabbed the bowl and another spoon. "Thank you, Dennis. I'll be back in a bit for my own dinner."

"Yeah, and maybe get somebody to check on that guy," he said. "Hate to see anybody suffer."

"I think he's done a lot of suffering and for a long time," she said.

"That was before," Dennis said. "Now he's here, and it's a whole different story."

Chapter 2

I T WAS UNUSUAL for Jessica to be as affected by a patient as she was by Lance. But something was just so frail about this big man who had been brought to these sad circumstances, and she found her heart melting for him. She checked up on him on a regular basis over the next few days, making sure he had food, water, and other drinks. Even between her rounds she found herself with excuses to go down that hallway to see him. Three days later, when she stopped in to check on him in the morning, he looked up and gave her a sleepy smile.

"Wow," she said. "With a smile like that, I bet you had girls dropping all over you."

"Maybe before the accident," he murmured, "but it sure hasn't happened since."

She chuckled. "That's because it was girls," she said. "Women are a completely different sort."

"What's the difference?" he asked curiously, as he obediently held out his arm for her to check his blood pressure.

"Girls are affected more by the prettiness on the outside," she said, "and women, at least women who have grown up and seen a lot of life, they know that the true measure of a man can only be taken from the inside," she said. "In a place like this, what we see all the time is that inner measure of a man."

He smiled. "I think I like that," he said.

"Good," she replied.

"But I don't have any illusions about finding a partner after this."

"Well, it's perfectly possible, and, from what I understand, it happens a lot around here."

"*Happens a lot*," he said slowly. "I know what happened with my friend Iain," he said, "but I assumed that was an oddity."

"Not only was it *not* an oddity but Hathaway House is getting a name for matchmaking." And she laughed.

"Hard to believe," he said, wondering if he'd made a mistake coming here.

"People here are not quite so shallow to just seek a quick relationship only. We see so much of what you guys go through," she said, "that, for those who fall in love, they already know who's on the inside," she said, "and that's worth everything."

"Sounds nice," he said. "I'm just not sure I believe that."

"Don't have to," she said. "You'll find out soon enough, just by watching the others around here."

"Only if I fall in love," he said, his lips twitching.

"Is that so hard to believe?" she asked, eyeing him with an odd look. "Do you really not expect to ever fall in love again?"

"I guess I just don't expect anybody to love me again," he said. "I don't consider myself much of a catch."

"That goes back to that hanging-around-with-the-girls thing again," she said. "For real women, it's all about the inside. Remember?"

"I don't know," he said. "I still think it's all about who'll be capable of protecting you and being there when the chips are down."

"Protecting and looking after are two different things," she said, her hands on her hips as she studied him. "And you're the one who's down right now," she said. "Helping you is a whole different story. Getting you back on your feet so that you're a vibrant contributing member of society," she said, "is what we're all about here. How you deal with the physical is the rehab, but how you deal with the emotional and the mental side of you is a whole different story. We see progress happen on one level, but then it stalls because it has to happen in all three areas."

"Does that make me a triangle or something?" he asked with a half laugh.

But she could see that he didn't really believe her. "It's okay," she said. "You'll see."

"What will I see?" he asked, as she walked toward the doorway.

"You'll see that your progress is important to move ahead on all levels," she said.

"I hope so," he said. "I'd like to think that the physical was the furthest behind."

She gave him a brilliant smile. "I hope so," she said. "I'm really looking forward to getting to know who you are on the inside." And, with that, she was gone.

THAT WAS A very strange nurse. At least in his experience, they rarely got personal. They asked questions about how you were doing, but they didn't really want to hear the answer. Yet Jessica appeared to be unique. But then, over his first few days at Hathaway, he had already realized the truth of Iain's statement about how different this place was. In fact, Iain wasn't even around anymore. He'd moved on, or rather he'd moved up and moved out. Maybe that was a better way of looking at it. Lance still hoped to see Jaden, and that hadn't happened yet either. Just then Lance heard the sound of crutches coming toward his door. When he looked up, there was Jaden himself. But it was a Jaden whom Lance didn't even recognize.

"Wow," Lance said, feeling older, frailer, and more broken than ever. "Aren't you looking vibrant and healthy?"

Jaden gave him a half smile and took several more steps inside Lance's room on his crutches. "Well, I am better," he said. "I still don't get to leave for a couple months yet though."

"You look amazing," Lance said, in shock. "I would have thought you were ready to be discharged."

"Not according to them," he said. Leaning over, he grabbed the visitor's chair, pulled it to him, and slowly, using the chair for support, sat down. "As you can see, I'm still moving pretty slowly."

"But you're moving," Lance said, "and that's nothing like what you were doing back at the old place."

"I know, and that's why, when I came here, I didn't believe Iain either. But now that I'm here, you realize that I'm halfway there—or, no, I'm probably 65 percent of the way there or maybe even 70, if I'm lucky. But Iain's like, good Lord. He looks like he's a bodybuilder or something."

"It's hard to believe," Lance said. "When I first got his email, I didn't believe him. I figured the joker would make a joke out of me, and I didn't want to be anybody's laughingstock anymore."

"Understood," Jaden said. "I have to admit that I was a

little concerned about that too. We all knew what Iain was like, but I don't think we understood that the Iain back then wasn't the same as the Iain right now."

"Is he really different?"

"Chalk and cheese," he said. "As in seriously different chalk and cheese. Before he was a joker, always making light of everything. Now he's seriously built, and he's got plans of setting up a center to help other vets like us get a new start in life," he said. "He's here with his partner, Robin, who works downstairs in the vet clinic. Robin's brother is even here," he said. "That's Keith, and he arrived about a month ago. Iain has helped him get on his feet a lot faster than I would have expected Keith to."

"Sounds like Iain has made a complete change in his life," Lance said. "That doesn't mean it's the same change that's available to us all."

Jaden looked at him, a smile playing at the corner of his lips. "And I think that's one of the realities we have to come to. We come with hope, but we don't really expect anything better. We can see that other people have done better, but we always expect that our recovery will be the one case that can't be improved upon."

Lance winced at that. "I have to admit that I've thought that a time or two."

"Of course you have," he said. "And things will improve. You'll be challenged physically. Your mind-set will be challenged, and your emotional balance will go off-kilter. Your physical balance will go off-kilter before it gets better probably," he said, "and there'll be this moment, before dawn, where you think it's not worth it, that you should never have come, and that it's all a terrible waste. Then you'll make this decision that you have to live with what you've got and have to stop monkeying around, wasting everybody's time, and just move on."

Lance stared at him in surprise. "Have you been through all those stages?"

Jaden nodded. "I sure have," he said, "and it's not an easy thing. But I've come out the other side so much better."

"Don't tell me that you've also got a partner," he said. "That I will not believe."

"Actually I do," he said with the gentlest of smiles. "Brianna. And that's something I really didn't expect. But the woman is fantastic, and, well, I mean, I didn't think this was possible, but she loves me too."

Instantly Lance felt jealousy spear right through his core. "I didn't expect to ever hear any of us say that again," he said softly. "I think, back at the VA hospital, we all expected to be alone for the rest of our lives."

"I did," Jaden said with a nod. "But, looking back, I wasn't fair to the other women in the world either. I assumed that nobody would want me because I was broken and would never be at the same physical level I had been before," he said. "Even with all the surgeries, I always assumed that I would never be as complete," he said. "Now I realize that I'm more complete but in a very different way, and the physical level isn't the prime consideration in my world. I've grown so much more on an emotional and a spiritual level," he said. "And I don't mean to go off all New Agey or religious or anything, and I can't really prepare you for what's still to come. All I can tell you is that a ton of change is available for you here," he said, "but it's a ton of work and not something you can just reach out and say, *I'll take it.* You must decide you're ready for it and see if you can make it all happen, but it's still not that easy."

Jaden stopped, shook his head, and said, "I'm not explaining myself very well. I guess what I really would say is just be open. Be open to whatever comes your way. Be prepared to work for it, and, if you do the job and show up every day and do the best that you can at this job," he said, "I promise you the reward will be way past what you ever thought you could have."

"Still sounds New Agey," Lance said with a laugh.

Jaden grinned. "I know. I tried to not sound like that, but it is what it is. You know?"

"I got it," he said, "and thanks. I'll keep it in mind." He motioned at the crutches. "At least you're on crutches. That's awesome."

"I actually can walk," he said, "but I overdid it yesterday, so I'm paying for it today."

"Overdoing it doesn't sound so bad."

"No," he said. "Overdoing it is what we end up doing sometimes when we keep trying to do stuff."

"I get it," he said, "and I can see that I'll have days where I'll pay for it too."

"Yep, there will be lots of those," Jaden said. "I tried to get down to see you over the previous days, but your door was closed a lot."

"The transfer wasn't very easy," he admitted. "So I kind of feel bad, but, at the same time, I accepted that I needed some adjustment time."

"You do," he said. "Have you made it to the cafeteria for food yet?"

"No, not on my own. So far the meals have been delivered."

"Well, I could coax you to come down to breakfast with me."

At that, Lance slowly sat up. "You know what? I wouldn't mind that at all," he said. "It feels too much like being a patient when you're in bed all day."

"It always feels too much like being a patient when you're in bed," he said. "Just like being in a wheelchair is much better than being in bed, and being on crutches is much better than being in a wheelchair. But, when you can finally put down those crutches and walk on your own steam and be totally independent," he said, "that is the very best feeling of all."

"I'm a long way from that yet," Lance said with a smile. He let his legs hang over the side of the bed. "These chicken legs," he said with a shake of his head. "I have more screws and metal plates in my leg—"

"I hear you," he said. "The thing is, around here, a lot of us are just like you."

"At the last place too," Lance reminded him.

Jaden grinned and said, "Yep, but what you'll see here is people making progress—not those who have accepted their fate and are just living with it. Many of the people here are striving for more."

"Well, in that case," Lance said, "if I can get off this bed and into that wheelchair, you can show me."

Chapter 3

W HEN JESSICA CAME to grab breakfast, she was surprised to see Lance at a small table with Jaden. But then again she shouldn't be because she remembered hearing that Jaden had put in a good word for his friend. Same as Iain. Apparently they all knew each other from a previous center. Better still, Lance had come down under his own steam. She liked that too.

As she stood here, studying his color, Dennis called to her and said, "You can't just stop there, mooning over people," he said. "My heart won't take it."

She chuckled as she walked toward him. "Dennis, your heart is already stronger than anybody's I know."

"Maybe," he said, "but you know I consider all of you to be my special ladies."

"And then you lose us, one by one," she teased.

He passed his hand over his heart and said, "Yes, and it's just devastating." Then he grinned at her and said, "What can I get you for breakfast?"

"I was going to have some yogurt and fruit," she said, "but I'm wondering if I need a bit more protein."

"How about a parfait with seeds?" he asked. "I've got chia seeds, pumpkin, sesame, and more fruit. And we could do a little bit of cheese on the side."

"Maybe I'll mix up something," she said. Walking over

and picking up a bowl, she started with fruit on the bottom, then yogurt. She added a heavy layer of seeds, more yogurt, and topped it off with fresh berries. She looked at it and smiled. "This looks perfect."

"Couldn't have made it better myself," he said with a chuckle. "You should enjoy that."

"I absolutely will," she said. Then she walked over, poured herself a cup of coffee and an orange juice, put a spoon into her bowl, and, with her tray in hand, she headed out toward the sun. When she heard a voice, she turned to see Lance, calling out to her. She walked over with a smile and said, "Wow, it's good to see you up."

With a motion to the gentleman across the table, he said, "I presume you know Jaden, right?"

"Yes, we've met several times," she said cheerfully. "Is it you we get to thank for bringing Lance out of his bed?"

"Hey," Jaden said, "I just invited him to have breakfast with me."

"And I'm glad you did," she said.

"I would have come earlier," Lance said, "but I was struggling with the whole getting-out-of-bed thing."

"Bed is an easy and comfortable place to stay," she said with a laugh. "So it only makes sense that you wanted to stay there."

"I guess that's the problem though, isn't it?" he said. "It becomes too comfortable."

"Often, yes," she said with a smile. "But that's not the issue. Right now the fact is, you're up, and you're moving, and I'm sure the rest of the team will be happy about that."

He winced. "So now they'll put me to work, won't they?"

"They sure will," she said, chuckling. "So eat your breakfast. Just don't eat too much."

"Will I regret getting up?"

"Had to happen one day," she said with a gentle smile. "And no better day than today."

And, with that, she picked up her tray again and headed out to the sunshine. If there was one thing she absolutely loved about Hathaway House, it was the location of the center. She could see the animals and enjoy the fresh air and sunshine. The food was great too, and it was hard to argue with very much about the place. She had worked in this field for some time and was thrilled to be working at this center that achieved such amazing results.

The fact was, she also got to meet some pretty special people, whether they believed in themselves or not. She had suspected that Lance would be another one who struggled with self-confidence now that his whole world had shifted. But maybe he'd surprise her. Maybe his problems would be something completely unrelated. She knew that, over time, they'd find out one way or another. This place was all about wiping out the false fronts and making the real person show up. Good, bad, or ugly, each was forced to deal with who they really were on the inside. Sometimes it was painful, and sometimes it was incredibly invigorating to watch. The bottom line was, she looked forward to seeing who Lance was on the inside.

"YOU HAVEN'T BEEN here very long," Jaden said. "Yet it looks like you've already got Jessica's attention."

"She's the nurse who's been looking after me since I first arrived," Lance said, by way of explanation. "Now that I'm up and about, I feel like I've been hibernating in my room. I'll have to kick that habit pretty fast. I don't want anyone to think I'm not pulling my weight or taking this opportunity for granted."

"Give it your best, and you'll move on," Jaden said. "The thing about Hathaway House is that only so many beds are here. So they really need to have people who will make good use of it."

"Right," he said, wincing. "Definitely time to get going on that then."

"Don't push yourself beyond what you can do," Jaden warned. "But, when you find you can do more, do more. If you give it your all, you'll leave here with no regrets."

"Glad to hear that," he said, and he listened to the words of his friend over the next few days, as he went through testing, testing, and more testing.

When Shane looked at him at the end of a session, he said, "You look disappointed."

"I guess I figured I'd be doing something constructive by now."

Shane laughed. "You are doing something constructive. Or I am, at least. I get it, but it's all about finding the starting point. In order to do that, we have to find out what's wrong."

"I would have thought that was pretty obvious," Lance said.

"To you, yes," he said, "but I need the details, so I can fix things."

"If you say so," he said.

"Have you met with everybody on your team so far?"

"Except for the shrinks, I think," he said with a mock shudder.

Shane laughed. "Everybody has the same reaction," he said. "Don't worry. Even the staff who works here have to see them twice a year," he said.

"Why is that?" Lance asked.

"Because our mental health is affected by being around all these patients all the time," he said with a grin. "But it's all good."

"So, these shrinks aren't something I have to be scared of?"

"I hope not," he said. "They're just here to help you. Remember that. And, if you have trouble and need a little room, just ask them to back off a bit."

"I wonder what they'd think of that," Lance said with a laugh. "I doubt if too many people tell them to get out of their heads."

"Actually I think a lot of people do," he said, "but it's all about setting boundaries. The thing is, it's better to set a boundary and to know that both of you can cross it, if you need to, than to slam a door shut and lock yourself inside. Because we can't help you if you're locked up inside."

"You aren't the first person to mention something like that to me," Lance said.

"Good," Shane said. "Give it some thought. So, I want to see you tomorrow at nine a.m. here, in shorts and a muscle shirt, ready to work."

"Is that a warning?"

"Not necessarily," he said. "Just letting you know that the testing is over for now, and it's time to go to work." He looked at his schedule and said, "Speaking of that, you're heading for the shrink today, aren't you?"

"Apparently," Lance said. "Dr. Monroe."

"He's new here," Shane said. "Let me know what you

think of him."

"Will do," he said, and he slowly pushed his wheelchair out of the large gym area and through the door. He stopped in the hallway and tried to get his bearings.

Shane called out behind him, 'Turn left and then take the first right."

"Thanks," he replied with a wave, then headed out, thankful for the assist. He got to a small office and knocked on the door. Almost immediately he heard a voice call out a reply.

"Come on in."

Pushing his wheelchair back, Lance reached forward, grabbing the door, then awkwardly managed to get around it.

"Looks like you made it after all," Dr. Monroe said, looking at him. "I wondered if I'd need to open the door for you."

"Apparently not," he said. "It was close though."

"Close is good because you still made it," he said, "and that's what counts. So, come on in and take a seat up at the desk. Just move that chair over, if it's in the way."

"Okay, I'm working on that," he said, and he wondered why the doctor wasn't helping him. Then he realized it was probably more testing. If there was ever anything this place appeared to really enjoy, it was testing their patience. He was a little tired of it, but, at the same time, he didn't want to show impatience because he figured everything he did would be suspect and questioned.

"There. Are you comfy now?"

"Good enough," Lance said.

"Okay, so now let's talk about you."

"Or we could not," he joked. "It'd be fine with me to

just let that slide today."

"Any particular reason you feel that way?"

Lance smiled, shook his head, and said, "I was joking, and I know perfectly well what this is all about."

"All about you. It certainly is," he said, "and lots of it."

At that, Lance winced and said, "You guys have such a bad name. It makes it all seem intimidating."

"I don't think it's deserved," the doctor protested. "Honestly, I'm a nice guy."

"Sure, but, if your job is to figure out what makes us tick and how to make us tick better, nobody really wants to get their head examined."

The doctor stared at him in fascination. "I like that analogy," he said, and then he picked up a pen and wrote a note down on the notepad in front of him.

Almost instinctively, Lance could feel his back tensing up. "What did you write down?"

The doctor looked up, a smile playing at the corner of his lips. "Your clock analogy."

Lance relaxed a little bit. "Oh, I guess that's not so bad."

"What is it that's so threatening about somebody writing notes for your file?"

"In a scenario like this," he said, "it's all about what you're writing about me."

At that, the doctor put down his pen, clasped his hands together, set them on his desk, and said, "Okay, so I won't write anything today. The last thing I want is to make you feel insecure."

"Too late," Lance said. "I'm on the opposite side of the desk. You're a doctor, and I'm not, so I already feel insecure."

At that, the doctor got up, walked over, shifted things

around somewhat so he could face Lance without the desk between them, and sat down. "Well, we removed the desk. What next?"

Lance stared at him in surprise. "Why would you do that?"

"Because it's not about doctor and patient or notes and files," he said. "This is just about the two of us. I need to know what I can do to help your sessions here be the most effective they can be."

Lance didn't have the slightest idea of what to say to that. Things had already changed from being a formal doctor visit to just two men sitting in chairs. He knew it was different, yet somehow it didn't feel that different.

"I'm not sure how to do that myself," he said slowly. "I've heard a lot of good things, but I guess I'm already afraid that I'll be the exception to the rule."

"Ah," the doctor said. "And that's always the worst, isn't it? I remember trying out for the basketball team in high school. Everybody else was good, and I'd always been told that I was good," he said. "Yet, when I saw everybody, throwing these shots up there and dribbling like crazy," he said, "it was just like everything went flying out of my hands, and I couldn't do anything. I tripped on the floor, if you can believe that. I couldn't shoot or even pass. I was a complete failure and figured I would be the only one who didn't make the team."

"Did you make the team?"

"I did," he said, "but not in the first tryout. As it was, later I was playing with a bunch of guys, just tossing hoops and having fun. Apparently the coach saw me, called me over, and asked me what had happened at the tryout."

"So what did you tell him?" Lance asked.

"I told him that I figured I would be the one who didn't make it. Sixteen of us were there that day, and he was only looking for fifteen. My own insecurity told me that I would be the one who didn't make it. So it was almost like a foregone conclusion, and I sabotaged my own tryout."

"That's an interesting way to look at it too," Lance said, listening to the words and feeling the shock in his heart. "Do you think I've already sabotaged myself being here?"

"I don't know," the doctor said with a smile. "Did you?"

"God, I hope not," he said. "I've barely even begun. I know that I'm afraid that I won't do well here, but I hope I haven't already started to make that a reality."

"What were your first few days like?" the doctor asked.

"Basically, a case of trying to hide away for a few days. I found the whole trip and adjustment a little shocking."

"And now?"

"I think I've adjusted," he said. "I've been through several days of testing, and I'm showing up for my meals and my appointments on my own," he said slowly. "Though we haven't really done anything yet."

"That *not really having done anything yet*, it's more of a judgment on your part," he said, "because I'm sure your team is gathering the information they need to put a program together for you. Which means that they're doing what they need to do."

"But it seems like I'm not doing anything yet," Lance said. "So your analogy just makes me feel like I've sabotaged myself and not done my part."

"Well, why don't we put that analogy off to the side for later, and you think about it as you go through the next few days to see if you're *actually* sabotaging yourself or if you're just waiting for things to get started and taking the time you needed to adjust being here."

"That sounds like a cop-out."

"Look. Maybe for the moment a cop-out is okay too," the doctor said gently. "We can't always be on, and we can't always be perfect all the time. So relax and take it one day at a time."

Chapter 4

F OR THE NEXT several days Jessica watched over Lance subconsciously, until she realized what she was doing. Then she accepted that she was doing it and continued. When she stopped in three mornings later, he was sitting up in bed, still in his pajamas, looking bleary-eyed. "Bad night?"

He gave her a ghost of a smile. "You could say that."

"If you need help sleeping at night," she said, "we do have sleeping pills and other sleep aids you could try."

He nodded slowly. "Maybe I'll take you up on it," he said, "but sleeping pills always leave me groggy and ugly in the morning."

"We could try some different brands," she suggested.

He gave a slight shrug. "I'll be fine."

"I'll take that to mean, *I don't want to take your drugs, so go away and leave me alone,*" she said with a laugh. "How did I do?"

After a momentary struggle, a smile emerged on his face, and she chose to take that as a success. Lance was definitely a hard person to read, and every time he shared something that was a bit more personal, communicating a little more freely this time than the last time, she felt like she'd been given the world. Somehow she was seriously hung up on this guy and didn't really even know how it had happened. "Are you coming for breakfast this morning?"

"I'll make my way to a shower," he said, "and then I'll probably come down. I'm feeling a little on the chilled side."

She looked at him in surprise, then quickly took his temperature and ran through the rest of her checks. "Everything is normal," she announced, quickly entering the info on her tablet.

"I think I was just sleeping without my covers overnight," he said, "and woke up feeling a little off."

As soon as she was done, she stepped back and said, "Okay, go have your shower," she said, "then get a hot breakfast."

He nodded and slowly got up, then, with the crutches, made his way to the dresser. Every step looked painful and slow.

She winced and asked, "Can I help?"

He looked at her in surprise, as if he hadn't realized she was still in the room. "Just getting clean clothes," he said.

She walked to the doorway and said, "Remember. If you do need anything," she said, "a button is on the side of your bed there."

He just nodded, and she knew that it would take an earthquake or another disaster for him to actually push that little button. With a heavy sigh she walked out and kept on with her rounds. By the time she was done, she was also hungry. She headed down to the kitchen and had Dennis make her a nice bacon and mushroom omelet, which she carried out to the deck. There she sat with her orange juice and omelet, relaxing and eating slowly. She heard voices behind her.

When somebody called out to Lance, she stiffened, then took a surreptitious look around to see where he was. He was sitting, hugging a cup of coffee off to the side, not part of the conversation, but there. His body language said that he wasn't included. He was backing away from everyone, leaning against the wall, as if he were too tired to stand up. She worried about that.

Because this was the first morning he'd been like that. She wondered if Shane had started to put Lance through his paces yet. That would certainly explain Lance being so tuckered out right now. And, if not, maybe it was just that bad night he'd had. When she got up and cleared away her dishes, he was gone. Saddened, yet going back to her office to add a few notes to his file, she wasn't surprised later when one of the doctors stopped in.

"Any idea what Lance's condition today was all about?"

"He said he didn't sleep well," she said, "but he just looked off."

"In pain?"

"Every step he took," she confirmed.

He nodded. "He's refusing painkillers."

"More or less declined the idea of sleeping pills too," she said. "At least when I suggested the idea this morning. And he didn't look very impressed."

"A lot of guys don't like to take their meds," he said.

"But are they mandatory meds?"

"No," he said, "but there's always that concern that, if they aren't sleeping, they aren't healing."

"I was thinking that too," she said. "I'll see what he's like tomorrow morning."

"Yeah. Good enough," he said. "But, if there's no change, this can't keep going on."

"Well, maybe he's up for yoga or some meditation," she joked.

"And, if that doesn't work," he said, "a lot of the guys do

well with the hot tub."

"I don't think he's been cleared yet," she said.

"Doesn't mean we can't get him cleared."

She kept an eye on Lance for the rest of the day, just checking in on his schedule and then walking past when she knew he would be back in his room. Once when she came, she got no answer when she tapped on the door. The second time the door was open, but he was sound asleep on his bed. Then it was dinnertime, and she was already off shift. She went back to her room, quickly changed, and headed back up for dinner. She was going into town this evening with some friends, a group from the center who would catch a movie.

After she was done with dinner, they met out front and went together in the same vehicle. She thoroughly enjoyed herself. One of the nicest things about working at Hathaway was making friends with the patients, but it was also nice to leave them and to not feel guilty about getting away. As health care professionals, they all experienced the same thing because it was doubly a problem when you lived and worked in the same space. They tried not to talk shop when they were out, but sometimes it was inevitable too. By the time she got home, she quickly had a shower and fell into bed with a smile on her face.

She hoped that, over the next couple days, Lance would have an easier time of it. But chances were, he would be stubborn and would not get along with the prescription drug program as it was. It's not that she was a huge proponent of drugs; she was a nurse after all, so she'd seen the benefits, but she also seen that some people didn't do so well with them. Still, it was always about trying to find out what worked for the individual patient, and that was something she needed to find for him.

When she got up the next morning, while doing her rounds, she headed to his room, but his door was shut. She knocked gently, but there was no answer. She went past, finished her rounds, and came back. The door was still closed, and again there was no answer. Frowning, she made a notation, then went in and had her breakfast. When she came back out, she walked past his door again. This time when she knocked, there was a muffled voice. She opened the door ever-so-slightly and poked her head in.

"Hey, sleepyhead," she said, studying him as he lay curled up on his side. He had a sheet up over his shoulders, but the blankets were on the ground. "Do you sleep so roughly all the time?" she asked, walking in and picking up the blanket.

"Only sometimes," he said, but his voice was groggy and his eyes only half awake.

"Breakfast is over, and you still have maybe half an hour before you start your schedule today," she said with concern. "I'm not sure who your first appointment is with."

"I don't know," he said. "I don't think I'll make it for food though."

"Tell me what you want," she said, "and I'll go get you something before it's too late."

He looked briefly interested in that and then sagged back and said, "I don't know. Whatever you think is fine."

She frowned at him and said, "You need to wake up and to get up," she said.

"I will," he said, "otherwise Shane will come in here and chase me out."

She laughed. "So, get yourself awake, and I'll go get you some food and some coffee." Not giving him a chance to argue, she headed to the kitchen. When she explained to Dennis what she was after, he gave her a plate of potatoes, with scrambled eggs and sausages. She placed everything on the tray, added some juice and coffee, then slowly made her way back to his room. He was at least awake when she got back.

He looked at her and the food with surprise. "I thought I had dreamed you talking to me," he said.

"Well, if I would be in your dreams," she said, "I'd like to think it's doing something better than delivering food." He flushed at that, but she just smiled, teasing him. "We were talking about you not having enough time before your appointment with Shane."

"I won't have time to eat all this either," he said, but he picked up a whole sausage on his fork and started munching. She turned and walked away. As she left, he called out, "Thanks."

She lifted a hand in recognition and laughed. But she was happy that at least he was eating. Now, if only she could understand what was going on with his sleeping problem.

LANCE WATCHED AS Jessica left, quite surprised that she had gone over and above for his comfort yet again. But then what he'd found was that she was one of those special few who seemed to really care about her patients. He was lucky that way. When he only had five minutes to go, he still had half a plate of food left. He pushed back his tray, got up, and got dressed awkwardly. Then he sat back down on the bed, had a few more bites of sausage and eggs. With a sigh, he realized he was good to go, plopped himself in the wheelchair, and slowly moved out. He heard another voice in the back of his head, saying, *Keep an eye on yourself over the next few days. See if you're self-sabotaging.*

He was sure he was doing this one thing: keeping an eye on himself. Yet he didn't know how to determine if he was self-sabotaging or not. Or was it he was afraid to hope? To hope for the one thing he wanted back in his life—music. Something he hadn't shared with anyone yet. Preoccupied, he went into the gym, where he was meeting Shane.

Shane looked up, saw the look on his face, and asked, "Heavy thoughts?"

"How do you tell if you're sabotaging yourself?" he asked quietly.

Shane lowered the tablet in his hand and turned to look at him. "Now that's an interesting question," he said. "Are you concerned?"

"I don't know," he said. "Maybe? Have you seen anything yet to say that I am?"

Shane grinned. "Nope, not yet," he said. "But I will be the first to tell you if I do."

"Good," he said. "I know Dr. Monroe asked me about it. Or rather, I brought it up, and then he told me to keep an eye on it for myself."

"In what way could you have been sabotaging yourself?"

"I don't know," he said. "I'm not sleeping for one thing."

At that, Shane frowned. "That's not good," he said. "Your body needs rest, and I need you to be awake and to be alert to do the work that we have to do."

"I just don't sleep," he said. "I'm tired. I go to bed, and then it's like my mind is wide awake."

"And I suppose you don't want to take sleeping pills."

"They don't agree with me," he said. "They knock me out, and then I wake up feeling heavy and lethargic the next day."

"Melatonin? Or other herbal supplements?"

"I don't think so," he said. "I was thinking about getting up and having a hot shower, wondering if that might help me get to sleep."

"That would be an interesting one," he said, "because, if it works, I'll have to make sure you have somebody with you. But there is a hot tub."

"For the evening?"

"Again, you must have an orderly with you," Shane said, "but it's not an impossibility. It's just not where we usually start."

"Right, so you'll ask me to do meditation and yoga and listen to tapes and things like that, right?"

"Obviously this isn't your first rodeo," Shane said with a chuckle.

"I didn't sleep at the last place either," he said, as he rubbed his arms gently back and forth.

"Are you cold?"

"I'm always a little chilled," he said. "I don't know why though."

"Interesting," he said. "Well, let's get you to work, and that'll warm you up fast enough."

Half an hour later Lance wished he was cool again because he was sweating like a pig, and he'd barely done anything. His legs were awkward and stiff. They wouldn't cooperate when it came to bending at the knee, but then, when he tried to push and straighten them out, they just basically rested against Shane's legs.

"I don't want you getting frustrated by this," Shane said.

"We have to start with where you're at," he said. "You can't progress if you don't acknowledge step one."

"Says you," Lance said. "I'm sweating like a pig, and I can't get anything accomplished."

"So, we'll change what you need to accomplish then," Shane said cheerfully. He had him back up in the wheelchair, and they gently did leg raises with his knee bent.

Slowly, with time, he straightened out that leg and did straight-leg bends, but trying to point his foot? Well, that was an impossibility. "It's like the ankle doesn't work at all," he said. "Too many plates and screws."

"The plates and screws," Shane said, "have nothing to do with the joints. They're all up in this shin bone area and up in your femur."

"So why is the ankle so stiff then?"

"We've got to get some blood flow into it," he said, and then he nodded. "And that might be something we need to do at nighttime too."

"What?" Lance said, missing a beat in the conversation and feeling foolish about it.

"A massage," he said. "But unfortunately it won't be a nice-feeling massage."

At that, Lance winced. "So, something that'll hurt again."

"Again?"

"I think everything has hurt for the last eight months," he said. "Not a day goes by where it doesn't seem like something is crying out in pain."

"Understood," Shane said. "Well, we'll start with this ankle and see if we can get it to move a bit." He walked over, grabbed some oil in his hand, and started working the ankle. But it wasn't a relaxing moment. It was painful, and, as soon as he worked some of the joint, he had Lance pushing against his hand, trying to force that foot to move and then straighten it a little bit more and a little bit more. At the end of the hour, he was sweating freely, but he could see that his foot had gained mobility. "I didn't think a massage could do that," he said.

"Often these muscles stiffen from disuse," he said. "You really have to work them all the time."

"I thought I was," he said.

"Nope. You're not walking very well," he said, "so these joints aren't moving very well. But we've loosened this one up a little bit," he said, "so I'll work on the next one, and that'll be enough for the day."

"How can you tell when the ankle has had enough?" he asked.

"The skin at the joint itself sweats," Shane said, "which means it's done. So let's work the other one, and then we'll keep this up over the next few days to see if we can get a better range of motion."

"You started on the ankles. Why is that?"

"Well, I'd like to start on the hips," he said, "but the ankles appeared to bother you and are slowing your progress for walking," he said. "So, we'll do it this way and then move up to the knees and then the hip joint."

"I would have thought the neck would have been one of the major ones," he said.

"All of them are major," Shane said. And he had Lance once again do a few exercises, pushing against his hand, trying to straighten that ankle back out a bit. Lance swore and cursed, but he pushed, and he pressed, and he worked it. And when Shane finally called it quits, Lance was surprised to see his ankle rotating slightly.

"So it really does make a difference," he said. "I'm surprised."

"All kinds of things make a difference," Shane said, laughing. "Don't be surprised. Just adjust your thinking at the beginning of the journey. There's a long road to go yet."

Chapter 5

TWO DAYS LATER Jessica walked into Lance's room to find him sitting on the edge of the bed, twisting and rotating his upper body. "You look a little better this morning," she said, pulling out her blood pressure cuff.

He held out his arm immediately. "I'm feeling a little bit better," he said. "Look." And he slowly rotated his ankles.

She smiled. "Is that a new motion for you?"

He nodded. "Feels like the kid in me has woken up a little bit," he said with a smile. "To be happy about such a simple thing, you know?"

"It is what it is," she said. "And it's new and different for you, so enjoy it and rejoice in the success."

"I think that's why Shane focused on it," he said, "so I could see a success. Even a small one."

"Lots of little ones pile up into a big one, and any success is progress, right?"

He looked up at her smile and asked, "What about you? What are your successes?"

"Getting through the day sometimes," she admitted. "I try to get away from Hathaway House every once in a while, just to remind myself there's a world outside. I went to a movie a few nights ago," she said, "so it's all about finding a life that works for me."

"What do you do in your spare time?"

She shrugged. "I like to write poetry," she admitted with a sheepish look. "Not fancy or anything but it makes me happy."

"I think that's nice," he said in surprise. "I don't know too many people who write poetry."

"Seemed like a whole generation wrote it all the time," she said, "then it died away. I've often thought about writing stories, but that seems like work, whereas poetry just flows off my fingertips."

"And that is probably the best way to have it," he said warmly. "Something that you enjoy doing but isn't too stressful."

She nodded and smiled. "That's what I was thinking. What about you?" she asked. "What do you have for hobbies?"

"I don't really have any right now," he said. "I used to play music, but I stopped when I went into the navy. I've been known to sit down at a set of drums every once in a while," he said, "but now my feet and hands don't work the same way anymore."

"You like musical instruments, huh?"

"I like music in general," he said. "I haven't found too many instruments that I can't pick up and play."

"Wow," she said. "I wish I could say the same. That makes my poetry feel pretty childish."

He looked at her with a frown and then shook his head. "These days, I couldn't sling two words together if I tried," he said. "In case you hadn't noticed, I'll tell you. I'm not exactly communicative."

She chuckled. "Yeah, I noticed."

But they shared a gentle look of understanding.

"I, on the other hand, can't possibly play any instrument," she said with a smile. "I tried to play the recorder in Introductory Music class when I was in elementary school, and that was just painful."

He burst out laughing at that. "Not sure I ever took *that* class," he said. "I probably would have enjoyed it, just relaxing, listening to the other musicians."

"And that just makes you weird," she said, chuckling.

"That's me," he said.

"Did you ever really get a chance to play?"

"When I went on leave," he said, "I had a favorite pub where I used to play the trumpet in the evenings sometimes. The trumpet is probably my favorite, but the guitar was always a good instrument to just sling around and have fun with in the evenings. Of course the piano is a favorite too." He looked at his fingers and murmured, "Or was?"

"Did you have other friends who played?"

"Long ago," he said. "I'm not so good anymore at making friends." He sank back onto the edge of the bed.

"Well, the music may change all that." She shook her head. "No lying down again. It's breakfast time."

He groaned and forced himself back up again. "I know I should eat," he said, "but honestly, my stomach isn't terribly impressed with the idea."

"Is that because Shane's appointment comes next?"

"Maybe," he admitted. "Some of those sessions are a little rough."

"But you can also tell him that they're too rough," she said.

"Maybe, but I don't want to seem like I can't do the job," he said slowly.

"Well, maybe asking him for smaller successes is a better way to go."

At the reminder of his earlier words, he looked up thoughtfully. "It's funny. Some things I don't really consider a success, like playing music," he said. "Because it came to me naturally so I didn't have to really work at it. But this? I really have to work at."

"Which is also why you need to ensure every success counts," she said.

"I'll think about it," he said.

"That's all any of us can do here," she said, "and what's important is to go at the speed that you can do."

"Got it," he said.

She took her leave, making the rest of her rounds, wondering how anyone could just pick up any old instrument and play it. When she thought about all the gifts she wished she had been born with in this world, that was always a sore subject for her. And playing the guitar, playing any kind of musical instrument, was one of them. Singing was another one. She didn't have that ability either. Her voice sounded like frogs with a cold; yet she found, with poetry, that words flowed off her fingers.

So, just like he said he didn't have to work for the music, she didn't have to work for the poetry. She did work at her nursing job, and she worked hard, trying not to get too attached to people and failing miserably. She could never be a foster parent for animals because she knew she would fail completely at that too. She'd want to keep them all.

Her shift kept her busy today, barely having time to eat a protein bar at her desk, but she wanted to eat in the dining room tonight. She had reached the buffet line right at a lull in the dinner crowd, grabbed a tray, and looked at all she had to choose from. She loaded up her plate, snagged a bottle of water, and found an empty table outside on the deck.

Just as she neared her table, she looked up to see Stan with this little white bundle of something in his arms. She immediately put her tray down on the nearest table and walked over to see what it was. And then exclaimed when she realized it was a puppy. "Oh, my gosh, what is it?"

"A Great Pyrenees," he said. "It was brought in after the mother was hit by a vehicle and didn't make it. We've got three of these guys," he said, holding it out.

It was the calmest little laid-back bundle of love that she'd seen in a long time, and she immediately wrapped it up and cuddled it close. It leaned into her embrace. "He's so beautiful," she whispered.

Immediately Stan handed her a bottle and said, "He's hungry too."

She laughed and offered the bottle to the little one, and he suckled quite contentedly. "Oh, jeez, how old is the little guy?"

"The best we can figure is about three weeks," he said.

"And why did you bring him up here?"

"Searching for volunteers," he said. "I've got two more guys to feed." He looked around to see if anybody else was close by.

"I can come down later too, when he needs another feeding," she said.

"They all need feeding," he said, "so, when you come, bring somebody with you," he said with a grin.

The bottle was soon empty; then she handed the puppy back to Stan and said with a smile, "You could have done that yourself."

"I could," he said, "but it's a rare experience to see a puppy like this."

"I'll keep that in mind when I come down. Let's see. What about eight o'clock tonight?"

"Eight o'clock would be good," he said. "No doubt somebody will be ready to be fed by then." Still laughing, he walked over and poured himself a cup of coffee. Then, with the beautiful little critter curled up in his arms, Stan headed back down to the animal clinic again.

She sat down to her plate of cold food with a smile on her face. Her table wasn't empty now. Lance had somehow moved in while she'd been busy with the puppy. She looked over and said, "You could have fed that little guy yourself."

"I wanted to," he admitted, "but you looked like you were having way too much fun."

"I absolutely was," she said, "but you can come down with me at eight tonight, if you want, and we can feed them again."

He nodded, the slow smile on his face just breathtaking.

And once again she realized it was another boon to her to see his progress, even just this way. He was opening up, unfolding before her eyes, becoming so much more of a person who she could spend time with than the original near stranger who had moved in here not long ago. He was so much more approachable now.

He motioned at her tray and said, "Your food's gone cold."

"It has," she said, "and I didn't even wash my hands," she said. "So that's also a no-no," she said, "but I'll have about half of this, and then I will go clean up." She quickly ate through her plate, then realized that he wasn't eating. She stopped, looked at him, and asked, "What about your dinner?"

"DENNIS IS BRINGING me something," Lance said.

Following the motion of his head, Jessica looked to see Dennis, walking over and setting a plate of ribs in front of Lance. He studied the ribs heaped high on his plate with joy.

She looked at it, looked at Dennis, and said, "I didn't see any ribs over there."

"Leftovers from lunch," he said. "But then you probably didn't get lunch, did you?" And his disapproving tone was impossible for either to miss.

"Possibly not," she said, "as it's been crazy busy today."

"Of course," he said. "Your dinner's already cold."

"My dinner is fine," she said. "I got to pet and to feed a puppy," she said, "so that'll always take precedence in my world."

Dennis nodded. "I heard three of them were down there. That'll keep everybody going for a few weeks."

"Stan said the mother didn't make it," she said.

"That's always sad, but we've got to get the puppies through six more weeks or so until they can eat on their own," he said. "Then I'm sure they'll find homes to be adopted out too."

"Is that what Stan does down there?" Lance asked.

"Stan is the vet who runs the clinic. They do a lot of volunteer work down there," she said. "And Dani is up for rescuing any animal."

"Which is hard to argue with," Dennis said. "It's always nice to know that we're helping the animals. And, if you're going down to feed the puppies tonight," he said, "check in with me, and maybe I'll be free to go along too."

"I'll do that," she said. And, with that, she stood and

grabbed her plate. Dennis tried to take it from her hands, and she shook her head. "You don't have to take my dishes too," she said. "Sit down and relax a minute."

He chuckled. "It's really not a hardship," he said. "I do it all day long."

"I know," she said. "So right now, I'll do it." And, with a big smile, she walked over and placed her dirty dishes down, then headed home.

Chapter 6

T HE NEXT FEW days, like every day, were full and packed. When she passed the hot tub at one point in time, delivering something downstairs, she saw Lance sitting in it. But his color was off, and he looked even weaker than normal. She immediately raced to his side. "Are you all right?" she asked, crouching down.

He looked up at her and smiled. "Yeah, I am. I've just been so cold all the time," he said. "Shane suggested I come out here for an hour and warm up."

"Why the chills though? Have they given you any medical explanation?"

"The doctor says my body is still recovering from the latest bout of surgeries," he said with a smile. "And my travel and arrival weren't as easy as I had hoped."

"I'm sorry," she said. "Most of the time patients recover from the trip and adapt faster than this."

He winced at that, causing her to immediately rush to explain. "Everybody has their own time frames for healing, and each person takes different steps," she said. "Maybe your arrival here was just a little premature."

"Maybe so," he said, "but I wouldn't have thought so." Even as she watched, he lifted a shaky hand to brush his hair off his face and to wipe the sweat out of his eyes. "Do you want a hot coffee or something while you're here?"

He chuckled. "Jessica, you can't spend all your time looking after me."

"I'm not." She smiled. "Besides, I've got plenty of other patients whom I look after too."

He sighed and relaxed deeper into the water. "I'm just trying to go with the flow, to not feel like a failure, and to not sabotage my own progress," he said.

"I've heard you talk about that a few times now," she murmured, sitting down on the side of the hot tub. "But, at this particular stage, I don't understand what you could possibly be doing that would be considered sabotaging your own progress. I just don't see it."

"I don't actually think I am," he said, "but I think it's the awareness that I could go down that pathway that's keeping me from doing so."

She sat back. "Ah, well, that makes sense." She smiled down at him. "How are the metal plates doing?"

"Aching," he said. "Shane wants to see more muscle built up around them to provide a little more protection around them."

"That makes sense too," she said. "He helped you a lot with your ankles. How are they doing now?"

He lifted one foot out of the water and slowly rotated it at the ankle.

"Oh, wow! It looks like you're doing really well with that," she said, smiling broadly.

"Yes, and no," he said. "The hot water is helping a lot."

"Some sun might help too," she said. "If you're always avoiding it, you're never getting any vitamin D."

"Maybe that's part of the reason I'm out here," he said. "It's just kind of weird to be in a hot tub out in the sun."

"But technically you're not in the sun because you're in

the shade," she pointed out.

"That's because I'll burn if I'm in the sun," he said with a laugh. "It's all about finding balance, I guess."

"Agreed," she said. "So, once again, can I get you something to drink?"

"No," he said. "It's all good." He shook his head. "Honest, I'm fine."

She nodded but said, "You're sweating pretty well," she said. "So don't stay in there too long."

He just smiled at her.

Feeling like she should stay and watch over him but not sure why, she headed back to her office, but it wasn't very long before she found herself heading to the cafeteria and looking out over the railing to see if he was still in the hot tub. When she realized he was gone, she sighed in relief.

Shane came up behind her, a cup of coffee in one hand and an ice cream cone in the other. She looked at the ice cream cone in outrage. "Where did you get that from?" she asked.

"Dennis. He keeps the ice cream in the back though."

"Man, I would love one of those."

"Just ask for it," he said. "So, who were you looking for outside just now?" he asked, his gaze watchful.

"Well, Lance was in the hot tub earlier," she said. "He worried me a bit because he was sweating so heavily, but it also looked like he was still in a ton of pain."

"It's taking him some time to adapt to being here," Shane said. "It will probably be another week or two before he's fully acclimated."

"Is it common to take that long to settle in?" she asked.

"It can be," he said. "It takes some patients longer than others."

"It feels like he wasn't ready to come," she said.

"Just don't say that to him," Shane said. "I think he was in this condition at the VA center for quite a while," he said.

"So he heals slowly?"

"His body has been through a lot of trauma," he said, "and each subsequent surgery added so much more. He had a bout of anemia too, which has really slowed him down."

She winced at that. "That makes more sense."

"We're running a bunch more tests too," he said. "We're not exactly sure if something medically is going on or if it's just that more recovery time is needed."

"I didn't even think to check his file to see if somebody was following up on that."

"I think his whole team is a little worried about him," he said, "but he's back in his room now."

"Okay," she said. "Hey, did you offer him an ice cream cone?"

"I didn't," he said, looking at the cone, "but you can do that. Go get yourself one, and see if he wants one."

She hesitated, and he nudged her gently. "Come on. You know you want to."

"I worry about him," she admitted. "Everybody else seems to be doing pretty well, but he isn't showing the same type of progress."

"Hence the extra tests," he said. "And, in fairness, he hasn't really gotten started yet. Go get him an ice cream."

She chuckled and happened to see Dennis wiping tables just then. "So, Dennis, what's this about ice cream?"

"Absolutely," he said. "What flavor?"

"Choices too? Man, you've been holding out on me."

He named a bunch of flavors, so she picked two and then said, "Can I get a cone for Lance as well?"

"Do you know what flavor he likes?"

She shook her head. "No idea. Just make it the same as mine." He raised an eyebrow at that but headed into the back. When she turned around, Shane was gone. He'd headed down the stairs and was even now cutting across the back pasture toward the fence where the horses were. She waited a few minutes for Dennis to return, and, when he showed up with two medium-size cones, she smiled, grabbed some napkins, and thanked him. She headed toward Lance's room, but, when she got there, the door was closed.

Why hadn't she thought of that before she came with both hands full?

She knocked awkwardly on the door. When he called out, "Come in," she tried to hold the two cones with one hand and open the door. She managed it but had to use her foot to push the door itself wide open. As she stepped inside, she said, "I know I didn't ask you about this, so I'm taking the chance that you actually want one."

He looked at her in surprise, saw the ice cream, and his face lit up. "I didn't even know ice cream cones were a thing here."

"I keep forgetting," she said. "I just saw Shane, and he had one, so I asked Dennis." She handed over the cone and said, "There were all kinds of choices for flavors, and I didn't know what to get, so I just had him get us two the same," she said. "So this is rum raisin and maple walnut." He immediately took a bite off the top, and she winced when she saw his teeth come down on the ice-cold ice cream.

"What are you wincing for?"

"You put your teeth right in the cold ice cream," she exclaimed. "I can't bite ice cream. So I just lick my ice cream."

"I can," he said with a shrug. "This is really good, Jessica. Thank you."

She smiled and nodded, then put a few spare napkins on his little bedside table and said, "I just figured you might like it after the hot tub."

"I really appreciate it," he said. He hesitated and then said, "I know they did a bunch of blood work on me yesterday. Did you ever get any results back?"

"I can check your files," she said, "but it'll take one of the doctors to give you the results."

"Of course," he said with an eye roll. "It's all about protocol, isn't it?"

"Always," she said. "Are you feeling worse?"

"Not worse, I'm just not feeling great," he said. "I think the doctors wanted to cover the basics to make sure it wasn't something other than just being tired."

"Okay, I'll check," she said and headed out of his room, wondering about the tests. As tired as he seemed, he really could be anemic. Also all sorts of bacterial infections could be going on. He'd had so many surgeries that his gut flora could also be completely messed up. As she headed back to her office to pull up his file, one of the doctors popped in and asked, "Did you happen to get the blood work back for Lance?"

"Not that I've seen yet, but I was just checking," she said.

"In that case, I'll wait while you take a look."

"That would be great because he seems anxious about it." She paused. "He could just be overtired, I suppose."

"Yes, it's possible, but I think more's going on than that," he said.

She headed toward her desk and quickly brought up her

computer, even though she was done with her shift. Logging in, she checked to see if any of the results were in. She nodded. "They're here, Doctor. I'm sending it to you right now." She added the results to his file and tagged the doctor on it.

Bringing it up on his iPad, he whistled. "Yeah, just as I thought, we definitely have an anemia issue." He looked farther down and shook his head. "Oh, wow. He needs to be on antibiotics like now."

"Ouch," she said. "Well, that might make him feel better in a way. To know there's a physical reason behind why he's been so down."

"He's noticed himself?"

"Yeah. I think more just feeling like he's not quite right," she said.

The doctor quickly changed the orders on the file and said, "Let's start giving him the antibiotics twice a day, and I want an iron supplement three times a day," he said. He shook his head at that. "We may have to look at some injections in his case too—or infusions even."

"You tell me," she said, as she walked over to the medicine cabinet. "I'll take him some antibiotics right now. Do you want him to get a second dose tonight before bed?"

"Yes," he said. "Then starting tomorrow, just breakfast and dinner would probably be the easiest."

With the best course of action sorted out, she quickly grabbed one of the little serving trays and said, "Do you want to come and explain it with me?"

He hesitated and then said, "Sure." Together they walked to Lance's room, just as he finished his ice cream. She pushed the door open a little wider and said, "Your blood work came back."

He looked up at her, surprised, and then saw the doctor behind her. "How bad is it?"

"Looks like you're running a bacterial infection," he said, "and you're anemic. I figured on the anemia, but the bacterial infection could have been the cause of it. So, it's iron supplements and antibiotics for the next bit."

"Great," he said. "There goes my gut again."

"Good point. So we'll add probiotics to that regime too," the doctor said. "I want you to get two doses of the antibiotics down today, so Jessica has your first dose."

She held them out with a glass of water.

He obediently took his pills and said, "So the second will be when? Bedtime?"

He nodded. "The nurse will come around at the eight-o'clock shift and bring you the second dose."

"Okay," he said. "Are you thinking I'll feel better after this?"

"Yes," the doctor said. "I think this is very likely the reason for your fatigue."

"I sure hope so," he said. "As much as I keep trying, I'm not getting very far on doing some of these exercises."

"The antibiotics will take three to four days to really kick in," he said, "and the iron supplements may be the same," he said. "It really depends on where this malaise is coming from."

Lance leaned back against the bed and said, "Three to four days then. Thanks for getting the results back so fast."

"They literally just came in," she said with a smile, then she turned and walked out with the doctor at her side.

LANCE HAD BEEN surprised when the doctor had wanted to do more blood tests. Lance remembered being in the hospital before, and it was just test upon test. But here at Hathaway House, he'd been feeling just low enough and rough enough that he'd agreed. And obviously there was a reason for it. It perked him up mentally too, since he'd been wondering if he was really all here or if he was just so spaced-out in life that he didn't have any effort to put into anything.

And that shouldn't be. He didn't want to talk to the doc about being depressed because that would immediately mean more pills. But, if the antibiotics and the iron pills were enough to make a difference, then that could really give Lance a whole new lease on life.

He sat up and shifted his legs over the edge of the bed because he really needed to get a real meal in tonight. His plan had been to go early and to come back early. He made it to his wheelchair and collapsed, feeling his body already breaking out in a sweat. That wasn't normal at all. He went to the bathroom, where he pulled the towel off the railing and quickly wiped down his forehead and the back of his neck. Then he headed out the door and down the hallway in search of food. He was one of the first to arrive.

Dennis looked at him, smiled, and said, "I gather you must be hungry?"

"I am," he said, "but I'm also really beat."

"I think some dark green vegetables for you," he said, "and some heavy protein."

He ended up with a steak for the iron and dark green vegetables to help boost that as well. Between the spinach and whatever cream sauce that was, plus broccoli with fried mushrooms and onions, and he figured he was doing just fine. By the time he made it over to a table, a lineup was at the buffet area, so he had literally just made it in time. He sat alone and ate quietly, as a group of other vets came around and filled up the table around him. He was pleasantly surprised. He was halfway included in the conversation and halfway not, and that was just fine because he wasn't feeling all that social himself.

When he finished his plate and put his fork down, he made his excuses, then slowly turned and headed back to his room again. He hated feeling quite so weak, but he was really feeling tired. The sweat broke out on the back of his neck again too. By the time he made it to his room, he struggled with the doorknob, wondering if he would even make it to his bed before he collapsed. When a hand reached out and helped with the doorknob, he looked up to see one of the orderlies.

The man looked at him in concern. "Do you need a hand?"

"I shouldn't," he said. "I've been fine all day. I'm just feeling pretty shaky right now."

The orderly stepped inside with him and quickly turned back the bedding. "Let's get you up here."

Lance nodded and, with the big man's help, slid his frail wasted body onto the bed and laid back. "They've given me new antibiotics," he said. "I don't know if that's got something to do with it or not."

"Or maybe it's the new antibiotics actually starting to work," he said.

"I've only had one dose," he said.

The orderly nodded. "Do you need anything else?"

"No," he said, "I think I'm fine. Thanks for the help."

"Remember. You've got a buzzer there," he said. "If you need help, call for it. I'll leave the door open," he said, "just because you're feeling rough."

"Good enough," he said. With the blanket pulled around his shoulders, he curled up ever-so-slightly and closed his eyes. It was only five o'clock, and he had no business trying to sleep right now, but his body was saying it was too tired to do anything else.

He opened his eyes to see Shane coming in and checking on him, and then about an hour later Jessica came by. Later on it was Shane again, and Lance muttered in a grumpy voice, "If all you guys keep checking up on me," he said, "I'll never be able to sleep."

Chapter 7

"**W**ELL, I'M BACK with your second dose of antibiotics," Jessica said with a smile.

Lance opened his eyes and frowned at her. "You should have been done working a long time ago."

"And I was," she said, "but everybody's a little concerned about your condition right now."

"I know." He hated feeling like he was causing everybody extra trouble. "But honestly, I'm fine."

"If you get a good night's sleep, you mean," she said, teasing.

He gave her a crooked smile. "Exactly."

She gave him his antibiotics, which he took with a glass of milk. Stretching, he used the remote to lay the bed back out again and said, "Now you can close the door and let me sleep."

"Well, I'll close the door partway," she compromised. "And, yes, you can go to sleep." She turned the lights down low, and he immediately closed his eyes and drifted off.

Outside, she waited until he was asleep and then propped the door back open again. She put a note in this file for everybody on the team to see, saying that he'd gone to sleep after his medication and was hoping to be left alone so he could sleep. Then she headed to her on-site apartment. She had been planning a surprise for him. She had picked up a secondhand guitar in town and had it tuned at a music store. The guitar itself had been dirt cheap, and she hoped it was good enough to actually play on. The tuning itself had cost more than the instrument.

But she didn't really want to hand it to him directly, so this was a perfect opportunity to take it to his room. So, with that in mind, she picked up the guitar, walked back inside the center, and put it in his room, being careful to not wake him. She left it just against the dresser, so he could see it when he woke up. And then she snuck back out again. She didn't want him to feel any pressure, but, if it would bring him pleasure, that was a whole different story. She was all about him getting more of that.

Back in her room she was restless herself. She headed outside for a swim and found herself plowing through the water. She knew it was all about being worried about Lance. It was frustrating to care this much. She loved and cared for all her patients, but, at the same time, it was frustrating to always worry about one continually. When she came out of the water and just sat in the evening air, drying off, Stan came out.

"Hey, how are you doing?"

"I'm okay," she said. "I just had to burn off some excess energy."

"Understood," he said. "I've got puppies that need feeding, if you want to come and give us a hand."

Immediately she hopped up and said, "Absolutely I do," and she headed down to the vet center with him. And there, one of the vet techs—Robin, she thought was her name— had a puppy and a bottle. As soon as she saw Jessica, she reached out with both and handed them off. Then she snagged up another puppy and another bottle.

"Quite a production line going here," Jessica said, as she curled up in a chair, cuddling the puppy. "They're so special," she whispered, holding the bundle of fur close. By the time the bottle was empty, the puppy was slowly falling asleep in her arms. She chuckled and handed him back. She looked over at the other two, but they were asleep as well. "So amazing," she whispered.

Robin nodded and said, "We're up twice a night with them," she said. "So, just like any parent, we have to cuddle them a little bit more often," she said.

"It's all worth it," she said, "because, when you care, when you look after them," she said simply, "they realize they are loved."

"Exactly," Robin said.

Jessica headed back to her room, smiling because just something about doing things for others made her happier. And, with a big smile on her face, she fell asleep.

WHEN LANCE WOKE up the next morning, he felt marginally better. He didn't recognize the nurse who came by with his medication first thing in the morning, immediately thinking of Jessica. Then he stretched, wondering if he felt better because of the antibiotics or just because he'd gotten some sleep. It was a hard thing to know. But at least he was feeling a little bit better. He also knew it would be pretty easy to overdo it and be right back where he was too. But he was happy to take this over the last few days he'd had.

Feeling a bit better, he got up, had a shower, and got dressed. When it was time for breakfast, he managed to get into his wheelchair and saw a guitar leaning against the dresser. He stared at it in surprise. Pushing the wheelchair closer, he reached out to stroke the long neck of the instrument.

"Well, this definitely has to be from Jessica," he said quietly. And wasn't that just so typical of her. She'd also been the one who had stayed on past her shift, who had tracked down the test results and the doctor, and who had given him his antibiotics last night, just to make sure that he got his treatment started. She was definitely somebody who cared and went above and beyond. It was such an odd thing. But, at the same time, it was really lovely.

She was a special woman. And maybe he was lucky enough to actually touch her in some way too because he certainly enjoyed every moment he spent with her. He just hadn't been feeling all that great since his arrival here, so it was hard to actually do anything for others. He let his thumb drift across the strings and smiled as he heard the notes that came from the instrument. It wasn't a high-end or an expensive guitar, but it had been tuned. He couldn't wait to play it when he got back from breakfast. Bolstered by the unexpected gift or loan or whatever it was, he resolved to ask her the next time he saw her, and he headed down to the dining area.

Dennis took one look and said, "Well, it looks like you got some sleep last night."

"You're right," he said. "I am feeling better this morning."

"Good," he said. "Now you need another good meal."

"That's what I was hoping for," he said. "How about lots of protein?"

Chuckling, Dennis made him up a platter of eggs and sausage, with bacon on the side.

"Pretty hard to argue with the food," he said.

"You'd be surprised," Dennis said. "Lots of people do complain."

"Well, that's hard to believe," he said. In his wheelchair, he stopped at the coffee station and tried to put some on his tray, but it was already pretty full.

"Not to worry," Dennis said. "I'll come behind you and bring you a fresh cup."

"Only if you've got time," he said, looking back at him.

"I'll make time," he said. "It's coffee after all, and we all need it in the morning."

Lance smiled and said, "Well, I sure do. I'm definitely a coffee drinker," he said.

And he slowly pushed his wheelchair outside in the sun. If nothing else he needed the sunshine and some vitamin D. Jessica was right about that. In the morning he wouldn't burn. He knew it would still take a few days for the antibiotics to kick in fully, but he had to admit to feeling a little bit better. When Dennis arrived with a cup of coffee and a glass of juice, Lance smiled and thanked him.

But Dennis just laughed. "Be prepared for company," he said, as he turned to leave, seeing Jessica coming with her own plate of food.

"One of the benefits of living and working here," Lance said, motioning at the food, "is that you get to have the same food that we do."

"And that's a huge benefit," she said. "This is actually fresh orange juice," she said, picking it up and taking a sip. She studied Lance over the rim of the glass, and he smiled back at her.

"Yes, I feel much better," he said. "I think I just overdid it yesterday."

Her gaze still watchful, she nodded. "And who knows if that iron is starting to kick in or not."

"I doubt if it's that fast," he said, "but I did make sure I had lots of dark greens and beef for dinner last night."

"Good," she said. "We'll get you there eventually."

"I just hadn't really expected the *eventually* to start off so dismally," he said.

"Everybody is different," she said. "Everybody has to heal on their own."

"I know," he said with a smile. "I'm just so grateful everybody came in and out last night, keeping me awake," he said, rolling his eyes. "But you guys were checking up on me, so I can't really complain. Speaking of which," he said, lifting his fork and pointing it at her, "I presume it's you I have to thank for the guitar."

Her face beamed into a beautiful smile.

He stared at her, fascinated, because she was one of those people who showed every expression on her face. Whereas he didn't seem to show any, she was like this open book.

"Yes, indeed," she said. "I remembered what you said, and I was at a secondhand store, so it didn't cost very much," she said. "Honestly, getting it tuned cost more than buying the guitar itself."

"Well, I did run my fingers across the strings," he confessed. "And it was nice to hear that it was tuned and in good order."

"Good," she said. "I never really know if people are doing what they said they'll do," she said. "And it's certainly not my field."

"Not a problem," he said, chuckling. "When I go back after breakfast, maybe I'll try it out." He flexed his fingers. "I'm not sure I'll be able to play."

"It's worth a try. Do you have sessions today?"

"No, not for a couple days," he said. "Shane has put me on minor stuff, no heavy-duty workouts until I'm back on my feet again."

"That's probably best," she said. "Much better to take it slow and steady instead of going too far, too fast, only to end up going backward."

"Exactly," he said. Just then somebody called her, so she excused herself, and he could see that she would not likely be back.

So, finishing his coffee, he rolled his way back over and filled it up again, tucked it into a little cupholder on the wheelchair, which he thought was one of the best little add-ons to a wheelchair that he'd seen. He slowly made his way back to his room. Once there, he put the coffee cup down, so it was out of the way, then picked up the guitar, trying to adjust his position. He shifted awkwardly up onto the bed, then shifted again so the bed was in a better sitting position, where he could sit with his legs stretched out.

Gently at first, he strummed the guitar. Soon soft gentle musical notes filled the room. He leaned back, closing his eyes, and let the pleasure of hearing the music float through him again, soaking it into his bones. It was such a healing sound for him, and he wondered why he'd never thought to have some musical instrument with him. Mostly because music had been out of the realm of possibility, so he'd just stopped letting it be part of his world. He gently let his fingers play, going from a love song to a country song and back to a ballad. By the time he opened his eyes, several people were in the doorway. He looked at them in surprise, his fingers coming down over the strings to silence them.

"I'm sorry," he said. "I never gave it a thought, but I

shouldn't be playing inside, should I?"

Dani stepped through the crowd to say, "Maybe not at certain times," she said, "but, during the day like this, something like that is absolutely beautiful," she said. "You are very talented."

He smiled at her. "Thank you," he said. "And I promise I'll try not to fill the halls with music all day long."

"You're definitely welcome to play inside during the day," she said. "But, when you want to take it outside, just let us know," she said. "I'm sure you'll have quite an audience who will enjoy the music with you."

He loved that. He loved the freedom to be a part of this. And he really loved the acceptance from those around him.

Chapter 8

JESSICA HOPED LANCE didn't see her in the back of the crowd, but she'd been leaning against the wall in the hallway with her eyes closed, just enjoying the music. When the crowd had swelled to the point that Dani was forced to step in, Jessica had felt a little guilty but not by much. She'd do anything to help this guy heal, and it seemed like the way to his heart was through music. Although the antibiotics and the new medications and supplements might just do the trick too, the combination of that with the music may give him a whole new lease on life. It wasn't always just the emotional or the mental setbacks but frequently also underlying physical reasons which caused somebody to not make the progress they thought they should.

When everybody had cleared out of the area, Dani stepped up, leaned against the hall beside Jessica, and asked, "So, was this impromptu performance your doing?"

"Am I fired if it was?" she said in a half-joking voice.

"No," she said, "but you've brought up a really good point. Music hasn't come up around here many times, but, when it has, it's been pretty important to those involved. We have a piano around here somewhere, but it probably needs tuning."

"He said he can play almost anything," she said quietly. "I thought I might find a guitar, and, when I happened across it, at a really cheap price, it seemed like it was worth a try."

"Definitely is," Dani said. "We'll have to set some hours and see if anybody complains."

"And maybe he can take it outside too," she said.

"As soon as he gets a little bit more strength in him, he will. It'll be months before he leaves, and it's obviously something that's good for his soul. Who knows? Maybe the music will be good for some of the other patients too," she said thoughtfully.

"The problem is," Jessica said, "there will no doubt be at least one person who complains."

Dani's grin was swift and lethal. "There always is," she said. "Anyway, good job." And, with that, she pushed off the wall and headed back to her office.

Jessica stayed here for a long moment, wondering if she should go talk to him. When she looked up at his doorway, she saw him sitting there in his wheelchair with the guitar in his lap. He just stared at it. She gave him a lopsided grin. "I was kind of hoping for another concert."

His grin flashed. "And I'd love to, but that would be pushing it," he said, rotating his shoulders to ease the strain. "And thank you. It was sweet of you to bring it."

She shrugged. "You're welcome. I'd like to see it help you on your path to recovery."

"It will," he said. "I know it. I'd forgotten how much I've missed it," he said, his fingers gently stroking the strings.

"We'll just have to see how much pushback there may be from other patients," she said. "Just because 98 percent of the place likes it, doesn't mean everybody will."

"I was thinking I should take it outside and to the pastures, where it won't disturb anybody."

"That's quite possible too," she said. "How does your afternoon look?"

"Sounds like I'm still on a reduced schedule until the new meds have a chance to work, but I am supposed to visit with my shrink this afternoon. And Shane for a short session this morning." He looked at the clock and said, "Uh-oh, I better get going." He quickly put the guitar gently against the wall inside the doorway and wheeled past her.

She called out, "Have a good one."

"Is that possible?" he called back, laughing.

"Sure," she said. "Why not?" She watched as he disappeared around the corner; then she headed back to the nurses' station. As she settled in, one of the other nurses huffed.

"Well, thank God that noise calmed down."

"You don't like music?"

"If I go to a concert or I'm at home and turn on the music, sure," she said. "But I don't like music rocking down the hallways."

"Oh, that's too bad," she said, "because music is really good for him. It's helping him to reconnect."

"There are other ways to do that too," she said.

"Such as?"

"Who knows? But everybody else has managed it without music, so I'm sure he can too. Maybe get him an iPod with earbuds."

Jessica laughed at that. "Well, that's another answer too," she said. "I didn't realize you were such a curmudgeon."

"I'm not," she said, "but I want music when I want it, not when it's not a choice."

"Good point," she said. As she sat here, she wondered if

she had done Lance a disservice, as it was obvious that they had already found one of the two percenters who weren't happy with his playing.

"I guess I sound kind of cranky, don't I?" she said.

"I don't know about that," Jessica replied. "I guess you have a right to how you're feeling. It's just kind of frustrating, since it was a promising step in Lance's recovery."

"Is he really that happy with it?"

Jessica looked at her. "You have no idea," she said. "It's seriously amazing to see the change on his face."

"Great," she said. "So I'll have to listen to that for the next few months now."

"Who in your life hated music?"

"Me," she said, "and it's because of everybody else who shoved it in my face all the time."

"And who was that?" Jessica asked.

"My parents, my brother, my husband. Everybody," she said. "It seemed like I was always surrounded by musicians."

And that gave Jessica an inkling of what the problem was. "And you don't have the same affinity, I presume?"

"No. God, no," she said. "I don't have the slightest bit of skill in that direction at all. It's really very sad."

"Maybe," she said, "but that's also life, isn't it? And you have plenty of other gifts."

"It doesn't seem like it," she said. "I spent a lifetime being the butt of jokes because I couldn't sing or play an instrument. It made for a pretty rough childhood in some ways."

"But you're an adult now," she said, looking at the woman who had to be in her late thirties. "Surely it doesn't still bother you."

Instead, Bridget looked over at her and groaned. "Even

my kids play."

"Of course they do. I'm so sorry," Jessica said. "Obvious-ly it's a sore point with you."

"Whatever," she said and forcibly turned her head back to the screen.

Jessica watched her for a few moments and then re-turned to her own work. It was an odd thing in life that some people were so happy around music, and others were just cranky about it. She suspected that Bridget's entire world being sucked into the whole music thing, yet feeling excluded herself, was the reason behind her bad reaction, but Jessica didn't want that to affect Lance's progress.

By the end of the day she stopped in to see him, but his door was closed, and he wasn't answering.

She checked in on him twice the next day, and he looked tired.

"I'm fine," he said, "really."

She nodded slowly. "Maybe, but, hopefully by tomor-row, everything will be looking better."

The next day he was perked up and looking much better again.

"You're looking a bit better."

"Maybe," he said. "I'll be doing my therapy work today, so we'll see how that goes."

"Just don't overdo it," she cautioned. Then she had to go because they had several patients leaving today and several new ones arriving, so she was rushed off her feet.

As it was, it was two days later before she had a chance to stop in and to really talk with him. "How are you doing?" she asked, bustling in, delighted to see some color on his face. "You look much better," she said warmly.

"Then I must have looked like death warmed over before," he said, but his smile was bright, his color healthy, and his gaze clear.

Even his disposition appeared a little more bouncy in her eyes. She checked his vitals and nodded with satisfaction. "Definitely an improvement all around." She watched as he slowly swung his legs over the side of the bed and stood, shaky but absolutely upright. She stood back and admired. "Don't you look fine," she teased.

He flushed but gave her a brilliant smile back.

"How's the music going?"

At that, the smile dimmed slightly. "Have to find a way to get outside because apparently, Dani has gotten some complaints."

"Oh," she said. "Isn't that typical."

"It is," he said, "but you have to expect, when you're in a place like this, that not everybody'll have the same relaxed attitude to music."

"Well, with any luck we can get you out at lunchtime."

"I was thinking maybe after work," he said, "like around four o'clock." He looked at her hopefully. "Want to join me?

"Absolutely," she said. "Where do you want to meet?"

"How about down by the pool?" he said.

"It's a date." And she skedaddled off. It just seemed like everything was so busy right now. But her heart was singing at the thought of meeting him this afternoon, even if the guitar was silent. And she barely had a chance to think about it again throughout the day until, all of a sudden, four o'clock came, and she dashed to the pool. When she got there, he was here with the guitar in his lap. Waiting. She smiled and said, "I'm here. I'm here."

He looked over at her and said, "No rush," he said. "I know you just finished work. I should have made it for fifteen minutes afterward to give you a break."

"Not a problem," she said. "I'm just grateful to be here," she said. "Let's go down and play some music to the animals."

He laughed. "Not sure they'll like that too much."

"You never know," she said. "I think all animals like a certain amount of music." And she walked with him, checking out that he was strong enough to do the actual rolling, so she asked, "Do you want me to carry the guitar?"

"No," he said. "I'm fine."

"If you say so," she said.

He just smiled and said, "It's all good."

"Great. So, whereabouts do you want to go?"

"Far enough away that I won't be upsetting anybody."

"I think the fact of life is that it's a little hard to please everybody."

"I just don't want to piss off anybody."

"Got it," she said. She pointed out where Midnight, Dani's horse, munched grass at the fence line. "How about down here?" she said.

He looked at the pathway and said, "How about we roll down a little farther away. I don't want anybody disturbed."

Surprised, she carried on walking with him, and, when he got to a spot he thought it was good enough, he stopped and said, "Dang, we should have brought coffee."

"We should have," she said with a laugh. "Next time we will." And she sat down on the grass and waited for him to get settled in. As soon as he did, she lost herself to the music. He ran through a full litany of what was probably old favorites, she didn't know, but she was stretched out in the green grass, her face to the sun, letting the breeze waft over her, as the music surrounded her and filled her heart with joy. When he finally fell silent, she said, "That sounds so lovely." She looked up at him. "Does it tire you out?"

"No," he said. "If anything, it's just the opposite. I feel better than I have all day." He shot his arms out. "The shoulder won't take too much more though."

"Are you still doing okay?"

"Yeah, I'm doing fine," he said, "but working with Shane is exhausting sometimes."

"It's *all* the time, from what I hear," she said. "You're not the first to complain."

"Well, you think that you know your own body, and then he shows you something that makes you wonder if you ever knew it at all," he said. Then he strummed away again on the guitar.

She followed his lead and just let the music rise up around them. She noticed that all the horses were coming to the corners of their pastures to get closer. And, even as she turned to look, Helga, the big Newfoundlander on three legs, was walking toward them.

"Well, it seems you'll have an audience, whether you like it or not," she teased.

He looked startled for a moment, then stopped playing and glanced around and saw the animals. "Well, look at that," he said with a big smile. "Who'd have thought they'd be so happy to see somebody out here playing music."

"I've heard that about a lot of animals," she said, "and I don't think these guys get to hear very much of it."

"No, there's a piano in the back of the big rec room," he said. "I saw it the other day. It's the first I actually remembered seeing it, but now I'm looking for instruments all over the place."

"Is there something else you want to get?"

"Well, I have several instruments in storage at my parents' house," he said, "if they've kept them. I'm not sure how they feel about being a storehouse for me."

"I would think, if they were your musical instruments, they would probably hang on to everything, wouldn't they?" She would at least. She couldn't imagine being a parent and not.

"They had to downsize here not too long ago, so I don't know," he said. "The biggest things to start with were drums, and I had several guitars."

"Well," she said, "when you finally get through rehab, you can add music to your list of things you want to do."

"I really would like to," he said. "How do you feel about seeing a guy on stage in a wheelchair with a guitar?"

She sat up slowly, then looked at him and said, "On stage?"

He nodded and frowned at her. "Would the wheelchair detract from what the guy could do?"

"No," she said. "I would think it would emphasize what he can do because he's doing something," she said slowly. "So you want to do live shows again?"

He gave her a boyish grin. "Yes," he said, "I think I do. My favorites are the jazz and the blues clubs."

"And why the wheelchair?"

"Just in case," he said, then switched topic.

"So are you tired?" she asked. "We can head back if you are."

"It feels so nice out here," he said, "with the breeze in the air." He lifted his hand and brushed the hair off the nape of his neck. "A haircut would be good."

"We have a hairdresser who comes through once a month," she said. "If you want to be put on the list, I can add you."

"It's probably not a bad idea," he said. "I'm used to having my hair so short, and, ever since the accident, well—" He shook his head.

"Do you have any scars on your head that stop the hair from regrowing? Do you want to keep it long enough to cover those?"

He looked at her in surprise. "I've got a couple," he said, "but I never really thought about that. I was just accepting that they were scars."

"With good reason," she said, laughing. "But a lot of guys are pretty touchy about it."

"No point in being touchy," he said. "My body is riddled with scars."

They slowly headed back, and this time she carried the guitar on her back, realizing it had a shoulder strap for just this purpose. And, rather than offering to help him push, she just walked beside him, keeping an eye out.

"You're very attentive," he said humorously.

"Well, I could say it's my job," she said, "not to mention the fact that I like to keep an eye on you."

He looked up at her, startled.

She shrugged. "Is that wrong?"

"No, not at all. I just wondered if you were like this with everybody."

"No," she said, "just a special few."

He laughed at that. "So I have competition here, do I?"

"Nope, not really," she said, laughing.

"Good," he said. "I'm not sure how I'd fare in a competition."

"Not an issue," she said. And then she hesitated and finally curiosity overtook her. "So, what about you? Are you in a relationship?"

"No," he said, "not at all. Haven't had one since before my accident," he said.

"And the accidents tend to break everything apart," she said. "We've seen marriages dissolve, and new marriages happen over what our patients go through."

"I can imagine," he said. "Though I can't imagine something like this splitting up a good marriage," he said, "but I think it would finish a rocky one."

"That's what we often see," she said. "A good marriage only gets stronger, as both partners pull together to survive it, and they end up doing very well," she said. "But, in so many cases, the other partner figures it's not what they signed up for, and they walk."

"That's got to be devastating," he said. "I'm glad I was single prior to the accident," he said. "I would feel like I was dead weight for somebody else to pack."

"Right," she said, "and I think that's how a lot of guys feel. Whereas it's actually the opposite," she said. "You come from a unique perspective with a strength that most of us have never had to find out if we have. You have found out who you are and are still working toward improving, while the rest of us go through life blithely unaware of how we'd handle such devastating and painful situations," she said. "Me? I don't think I could handle this like you have, and I've certainly seen a lot of others who can't. But, when I see the guys and gals here working so hard—and I see how they progress in their recovery and how they walk forward in whatever form they have to walk forward with—it just makes my heart smile. You guys are just so awesome."

He chuckled. "That's not exactly how most of us would view ourselves nowadays."

"That's sad. It is," she said. As they approached the center, Stan whistled and called out, waving her over. She looked over at Lance and said, "Let me go talk to Stan for a few minutes."

"Just pass me my guitar," Lance said. "I'll go up to my room for a little bit," he said. "I'm a little more tired than I expected."

She looked at him and frowned.

He waved her off. "I'm fine."

"If you're sure?"

"Go on," he said.

LANCE WATCHED AS Jessica dashed into the vet clinic, then made his way to the elevator. Once he was alone, he got inside and sank into his wheelchair. He'd pushed it too far and was paying for it, but he didn't want to ask her for help. Pride was a strange thing, but he would survive. Upstairs on his floor, he slowly made his way to his room. He put the guitar down, closed the bedroom door, and slowly made his way onto the bed. As he collapsed onto the bed, he thought he heard somebody at the door. "I'm just lying down for a bit," he called out.

Shane stuck his head around the door. "I saw you come down the hallway." He came in, took one look, and said, "How's the arm, that shoulder?"

He just glared at him. "What about them?"

"Did you think I wouldn't notice? Playing the guitar will tax that shoulder," he said. "It's already stripped of some very important muscles."

Slowly Lance sagged in bed. "I was really hoping it

would be fine," he said. "But every time I play—"

"I know," Shane said, coming over and taking a look at the shoulder. "Stretch out on your stomach," he said. "Let me work it over a bit and see if we can loosen up some of the tension there. I hadn't realized music was a big part of your life."

"And it could be a big part of my future," Lance said, "but only if I can play without hurting myself." They stretched the bed out totally flat, and, with Shane's help, Lance flipped over onto his belly and tried to relax. He knew this arm was pretty ugly, but it was the one that he used to pick the guitar strings.

"Have you tried any other instrument?"

"Haven't had access to anything," he said. He waited while Shane put something on his hands, and then, slowly, working from the center of the scapula over the shoulder bone and down the elbow into the hand, he massaged each and every one of the muscles. "Some of the muscles back here are in rough shape," Shane said. "It looks like we need to do some extra work on those."

"Well, I wasn't really thinking of music when we did our initial assessments," he said. "At the time, I wasn't even sure I could still play."

"Yeah, but now that I know, we'll put in some extra time and see if we can get this shoulder to work," Shane said. "It's just as important that we have our pursuits and the things that matter to us, as well as being fundamentally functional."

"Well, it worked," he said, "but it was awkward being in the wheelchair and having to hold everything differently. So I strained the shoulder."

Shane didn't say anything, so Lance kept quiet and just

let him work. By the time he finished working on the arm, it still ached, but in a good way. It was much better than when he first came back from being outside. "Pushing the wheelchair back to the center wasn't very helpful either," he murmured.

"No, I heard the music and saw you out there," Shane said. "I guess you were trying to get away from bothering others, huh?"

"Dani said there have been a few complaints," he said.

Shane sighed. "As much as I like people, sometimes I don't like people. But everybody is different, so not everybody may have appreciated the impromptu concert."

"Exactly," he said, "and I don't have a soundproof room, and that's way too expensive to do here. So, as long as I can find a place to go and do some playing every once in a while," he said, "I figure at least I can stay in touch and try and build up the arm."

"Not playing too much too quickly would also help," Shane said. "Remember. We've got to do things in stages."

"I guess I'm impatient. I saw the guitar, picked it up, and I played, never thinking it would be stopped the next day."

"So today is what? Three days since the last time?"

"Yes," he said. "I thought it would be fine."

"And you thought that, if you were far enough away, it wouldn't matter if you made a mistake, since nobody would really be listening, right?"

That prompted a surprised laugh from Lance. "I guess you could say that. I didn't think Jessica would really mind."

"She looked totally happy to me," Shane said.

"Yeah, but sometimes I think she's there as a nurse, an overcompensating nurse in some ways," he said. "I can't really explain it."

"Listen, Lance. We all have a challenge," Shane said, "of separating our personal feelings from our professional feelings. What I can tell you is that this is the first time I've ever seen her get so involved with a patient."

"Seriously?"

"Seriously," Shane said. "Now let's do some work on the other side," he said. "We can't have you lopsided." He quickly worked the other shoulder and scapula, then all the way down to the fingers. When he was done, he tucked that shoulder back under the sheet. "Now, if you can power nap for a few minutes, do so," he said. "Otherwise, when you get up, have a hot shower to keep those joints rotating," he said, "and we'll be adding that to our work list."

"Sounds good," he murmured.

And Shane just chuckled. "You're almost asleep as it is," he said.

"I am. I didn't expect it, but I am."

Chapter 9

TWO DAYS LATER Jessica saw Lance at lunchtime.

He looked up in surprise when she sat down quickly at his table. "You look rushed."

"It's been crazy," she exclaimed, brushing loose tendrils of hair off her face. "We're short-staffed again, so we're all doing double duty, trying to keep things afloat."

"That's always tough."

She watched him eat. "You're favoring your shoulder." He frowned at her. She nodded. "I can see it." He just glared. She shrugged and said, "Fine, don't tell me," she said. "I'll just have to guess what happened."

"Nothing happened," he said.

"If you say so," she said.

But, as she studied him, he knew it wouldn't be long before she said something. Finally he caved instead of arguing and said, "The guitar playing put a bit of a strain on my arm."

Immediately she leaned across the table and whispered, "Seriously?"

He nodded. "I should have expected it," he said. "Really. I mean, I haven't played in a long time and was using muscles that I'm not used to using."

"I never even thought of that," she whispered. "I'm so sorry."

"It's not your fault," he said, laughing. "And, since I know now, I can do what I need to do," he said.

She nodded. "So, no more impromptu concerts?"

He laughed. "Not for a few days at least."

"Okay," she said. "I can live with that. The piano is in the other room."

"Yeah, I saw it. Looks like it hasn't been played in a while," he said.

"Dani told me that it's been there for a long time and that it needs to be tuned," she said.

"Well, if I can't play the guitar," he said, "chances are I can't play the piano very much either."

She looked at him, nodded, and said, "I'm sorry. I didn't even think of that."

"It's okay," he said. "With Shane's help I might actually get there."

"So, Shane knows?"

He winced. "No way Shane couldn't know."

"Oh, my gosh," she said. "That bad, huh?"

"Or that good," he said, laughing again.

"As long as you haven't permanently hurt yourself," she said, worried and feeling guilty.

"Nope, even better," he said. "He'll add this to my training plan."

"That's awesome," she said. "That's so great to hear." She smiled broadly. "That's huge news actually."

"Well, it's one more thing to work on," he said. "I don't know what kind of news it is, but it gives me something to work toward that's very close to my heart."

"And, if that's the case," she said, "you'll work that much harder in order to get something back that you really want for yourself. That Shane is a pretty wily one."

Lance laughed, then smiled and said, "And you're a great cheerleader."

"I'm not sure about that," she said, "but everything I do comes from the heart." She nodded. "All of us want the best for you here."

"And that," he said, "is worth everything. So thank you."

LANCE WATCHED AS Jessica bounced away, almost as fast as she had come. He'd wondered what was up when he hadn't seen her as much, but hearing they were short-staffed made a lot of sense. He'd noticed other people were a little frenzied at times too. He finished up his lunch and slowly made his way back to his room. His morning session had been a bit rough, but, then again, it was his fault because of the guitar work.

As he stopped, he checked his tablet to see what was next on his day and then groaned because it was Dr. Monroe for a shrink visit. When it was time, Lance made his way, wheeling himself toward the office with a full cup of coffee. When he got to the outer office, he pushed the button to say he was here, and the door opened almost immediately.

Dr. Monroe looked at him, smiled, and said, "Come on in." As Lance made it in without spilling the coffee, Dr. Monroe laughed and said, "Well, that's a new trick."

"Seems like I needed some," Lance said with a smile.

"From what I've been hearing up and down these hallways, you've come up with a few tricks of your own. The guitar playing was a surprise. You're pretty good."

Just enough admiration was in his tone that Lance perked up. "I hope it didn't disturb you," he said. "I guess I went a little overboard in my joy of playing again."

"You should never apologize for having so much fun with a talent like that," he said. "Clearly you are very gifted."

"Well, if I can get back to it full-time, that would be a huge boon," he said, "but the jury is out on how the muscles will handle it. They aren't doing too well so far, but Shane has added some extra exercises to my program."

"Does it need to be full-time?" Dr. Monroe asked, as he walked around the side of his desk and sat down. "You never mentioned music at all before."

"I think I had shut off that part of my life," he said. "I could tolerate only so much grieving and loss at once, and that just got lumped in with the rest of what I had lost."

"And yet you haven't, have you?" he asked. "Lost your talent?"

"Maybe not. I'm interested in trying other instruments now too," he said. "I'm hoping I can find one that doesn't put such a strain on my muscles."

"Or some that you can build up to," the doctor said with a laugh.

Lance gave him a crooked smile. "That too."

"Are you thinking you can parlay something into full-time work?"

"Potentially," he said, turning to stare out the window. "I used to play at a club, way back when, focused on jazz and blues," he said. "I guess a part of me wonders if I could make enough of a living doing that in the evenings to not have to find a full-time nine-to-five job."

"Well, you'll get your benefits, so maybe that is something that you could do to make enough to tide you over."

"Yeah, I don't know," he said. "Back then the tips were more than the actual wages, and that helped me get where I needed to go."

"Do you remember what the tips were like?"

Only curiosity was in the doctor's voice, so Lance answered with the same tone. "Hundreds a night," he said. "I have no idea what it would be now."

"If you built up a decent following," Dr. Monroe said, "even working just Friday and Saturday nights, you could probably pick up five hundred a weekend then, right?"

"Probably twice that," Lance said. "At least on a good weekend."

"Lance, that's four thousand a month," he said in surprise.

"Puts it in perspective, doesn't it?" he said, staring down at his arm, opening and closing his fingers. "It just depends on whether I can get good enough to play at a club again. And whether I can do several hours of music without damaging myself."

"That's something to talk to Shane about for sure, so you have realistic expectations and all, but that really seems like a legitimate goal to work toward," he said. "And, from what I heard, you're definitely good enough to play at a club."

"Maybe," he said, "but there's a lot of competition for gigs like that. I used to play, mostly jazz. I do love my blues too."

"I'd love to hear that," Dr. Monroe said. "Actually a lot of us here love jazz. And we have a couple good jazz and blues clubs in town. Maybe you should send out a call and ask what they do for live music gigs."

Lance considered it and then nodded. "Maybe down the road," he said. "No point jumping into something that I can't achieve, like if Shane can't get the muscles to the point of being able to play for several hours."

"Meaning?"

He looked at him in surprise. "Meaning, I just don't want to jump the gun."

"Got it. Just keep in mind that, if you do get some interest going, it might help you work harder toward that goal."

"Not sure I need somebody else's interest to work harder," Lance said. "I'm not sure you understand how much of a new lease on life I already got just because I can play some music. If I can only do a half hour or a few songs a day, it's still a few songs a day."

"Right," he said, "but, from what I'm hearing, you've been playing for a lot more than half an hour."

"I have," Lance admitted, "but with pretty rough repercussions. Today I'm fairly sore from the workouts we started doing to try to build up the shoulder muscles. I wouldn't want to pick up the guitar and play at all today," he said. "My mind and heart want to, but the muscles are screaming at me already."

"And I hope you're listening," the doctor said.

Lance nodded. "Oh, I am. Trust me on that."

"So, if this is giving you a whole new lease on life, it appears that you're also thinking about your future."

"I started thinking about that after meeting Jessica," he said with a laugh. "Nothing like seeing a beautiful woman to make you wonder about your own future."

Dr. Monroe sat back with a smile and a twinkle in his eyes. "You're right there," he said. "And?"

Lance's eyebrows shot up. "And what?"

"Did you come to any conclusion?"

"Nope. Not at all," he said. "She's a stunning woman and really dedicated to her work here and to her patients."

"I hear a *but* in there somewhere," the doctor said, leaning forward. "Are you afraid that she sees you only as a patient?"

Lance winced. "You like to go right for the jugular, don't you, Doc?"

"Not necessarily," he said, "because it's all about balance and about you finding goals you can live with."

"Maybe, but it's also about finding goals that are doable," Lance said. "I don't want to go down that direction if it doesn't look like I can go the distance."

"Interesting turn of phrase," the doctor said. "Go the distance *yourself*, you mean? As in, having relationships, intimacy, even marriage? Or going the distance, as in, *she* might not like you well enough to stand the test of time and of distance?"

"I don't know," he said. "I guess I'm just not really sure what it is I was looking at doing at this point. The whole music idea had been tabled for a while, so it's kind of a new idea," he said. "Besides, I would also like to think I wouldn't head down that pathway if there weren't signs from Jessica that she was walking beside me," he said. "As for *more* than that, there doesn't seem to be any reason why I can't have a long fulfilling intimate relationship with the right partner," he said.

Just the thought of it filled him with a shiver of delight. When he had first woken up in the hospital, he had figured *that* life as he'd known it was over. But apparently not. Nothing filled him with happiness more than to know that he could walk down that path and find somebody who would love him for who he was now. "It feels very different though," he said.

"In what way?"

"Because before I was looking for different things," he said. "Now it seems like I'd be happy to get so much less."

"Is it less though?" the doctor asked. "Or is it not so much about less or more but instead about the basic foundational things in life. Like being loved for who you are."

"Did you read my mind?" he said with a chuckle. "Before, in my life, I had plans for all these different things in a relationship," he said. "Yet I didn't even really plan. I was just happy to have somebody to go out with, happy to have somebody interested in doing things together, wanting the same things." Abruptly he stopped and frowned.

"How is that different from right now?" Dr. Monroe asked.

"In many ways it isn't," he said quietly. "I guess the only real difference is that I'm not the pretty boy I was, and I have some physical challenges now," he added quietly. "And whoever came into my world would have to accept all that."

"Do you think that somebody coming into your world would be perfect?"

"Nobody is perfect," he said.

"Exactly. So, whoever you end up having as a partner will have challenges too, and you'll be prepared to work with them, aren't you?"

"Of course," he said. "That's just part of the deal, right?"

"It absolutely is," the doctor said. "So, in the end, it's really not that different now versus before, is it?"

"It feels different," he said slowly.

"Yes, but only because you're feeling differently about who you are," the doctor said with a gentle smile.

Lance nodded. "Obviously I'm not the same person I was."

"No," the doctor said. "You're better." Lance looked at

him in surprise, but the doctor nodded. "Lance, what you're saying is something I've heard many times over. We get all these strong strapping young men who have been cut down in the prime of life and are working to rebuild their lives into something that, for them, seems *so* different," he said. "But, at the end of the day, what we really want is to be loved for ourselves. We want to be accepted for ourselves. We want somebody to care about who we are. And it doesn't really matter about what anybody else may think, other than that one special someone."

"Wow. Very true," Lance said. "So, you're right. I guess I don't want anything different, except that I want somebody to see me for who I am now."

"And, in this way," the doctor said, "what they'll see is literally what they'll get. You're a much more honest and open person now, just because life has given you enough lemons to make lemonade, as they say, but you still have the peels and the wreckage around you. So, anybody who loves you now will love you for who you really are on the inside."

"Does that mean my physical body is so hard to love?"

"Not at all," the doctor said. "But the physical becomes secondary. Not the primary focus."

"But sexual interaction is good," Lance argued.

"It's divine," the doctor said with emphasis. "And a very welcome part of any long-term relationship. And honestly, I've seen that lovemaking happens many times too, yet I don't think it has as much to do with the physical attraction. I think it has to do with that special *spark* between two people, and, once that spark is there, the physical just becomes a conduit for the emotions. And, more often than not, the physical body, the aesthetics of it, makes no difference."

"I hope so," Lance said, "because otherwise it'll be a little tough to find anybody who'll like this." And he motioned at his body.

"Looks to me like you're already well on your way," the doctor said with a big grin.

Lance realized the doctor meant Jessica, and Lance felt something settle inside himself. "Maybe and maybe not," he said, "but I'm grateful that I can even talk about this right now and can even think that potentially she's there on the same pathway with me."

"Exactly," the doctor said.

Chapter 10

JESSICA'S DAYS CARRIED on in a regular pattern of constant work. Visiting with Lance, more work, visiting with Lance, a couple trips into town for a breather, and more work. Finally, after a week had gone by, they were back up to full staff again. She walked with a cup of coffee down the hallway to check in on Lance. It was early yet, ten minutes before her rounds were due to start. She knocked on his door and heard him call out. Opening the door, she stepped in, and he looked up in surprise.

She smiled. "I know I'm early," she said. "I just somehow ended up at work a little bit too early, so I have time for a cup of coffee and thought I'd stop in and say hi." His smile was real, and she loved that about him.

"You know you're always welcome here," he said. He dropped what was in his hands.

Looking at it, she asked, "Sheet music?"

He nodded. "It is," he said. "I used to write music too."

He gave her a lopsided grin that reminded her of a little boy caught doing something he wasn't supposed to. "Wow," she said in awe. "You really are multitalented, aren't you?"

"Well, I was," he said. "Trying to get the fingers to do what I need the fingers to do now? Well, that's a different story."

"But you don't have to figure it all out right away, do

you?"

"No," he said. "Not necessarily. As long as I'm figuring it out and making progress."

"That's true." She smiled at him. "I didn't bring you a cup of coffee because I wasn't sure if you were ready or not."

"I'll get one when I head down for breakfast," he said. "I was just looking at some songs and wondering if I wanted to try writing again."

"Well, if you need anything," she said, "just ask."

"Thank you," he said. "I might." He looked down at the pages, picked them up, and tucked them into the bottom of a big notebook he had.

"Is that a special song?"

"Not really," he said. "It's one I've been working on for a long time."

"That means it's definitely special then," she said. She looked at her watch and groaned, hopping to her feet. "Honestly, the time whips by when you've got to head to work."

He laughed. "The time just whips by, period."

She waved at him and headed to her office. Once there, she sat down and started her day.

Shane popped his head in a couple hours later and asked, "Have you talked to Lance at all?"

"This morning for a minute," she said, looking up from her computer monitor. "Why? What's the problem?"

"No problem," he said. "His hands are definitely strengthening up nicely. The shoulder needs more work, but it's getting there too."

She beamed. "That's great," she said. "I know he's been quite concerned about playing music."

"Not only playing music," Shane said, "but apparently

our boy is very talented and actually has played in several bars and clubs."

She looked at him in surprise. "He mentioned that. I'm not surprised, as he does seem to hold an audience."

"I was hoping that maybe we can get a little more music back into his life, but we still have some patients and staff who don't find it appealing," he said.

"I was thinking about asking Dani if maybe on Saturday or Sunday he could have an hour, and they could shut their doors and ignore him for that sixty minutes."

"That's not a bad idea," he said. "To schedule it ahead of time, so they can deal with it however they choose."

She nodded. "He does go down to the pastures a fair bit," she said. "I know the animals are really enjoying that."

He laughed. "Still, it would be nice if we could hear it too," he said enviously. "I know we can't do it late in the evening or in the afternoon when people are sleeping or napping, but maybe four or five o'clock before dinner."

She nodded. "Let me talk to Dani about it." He nodded and disappeared. When she was done with rounds, she stopped by Dani's office and mentioned what Shane had said.

"You know what? I was thinking about that too," Dani said. "I'd love to hear more live music, though I know that we do have some people who aren't terribly happy about it, but, if we gave them specific times and alternatives, then it's something they could plan for. But we should pass it by Lance first though," Dani said.

"I'm sure he'd be fine with it but—"

"But I think we should pass it by him," Dani said, laughing. "And, by the way, I'm getting the piano tuned too."

"Wow," she said. "You know something? Once you do that, you may find you've got a bunch of musicians in the place."

"And that would be fine by me," Dani said. "I think music is good for the soul. Particularly for anyone like Lance. Getting it back in his life could be a huge motivator."

"Agreed," she said. "So let's hope this works out with everybody."

"ARE YOU SERIOUS?" Lance looked at Dani in delight. "I'd love to have an hour to play on Saturday. I mean, I'd take two or three if I could," he said, as he held up his hand. "I know an hour is already a lot."

"It's not a lot for anybody who likes live music," Dani said with a smile, "but it's a lot if you hate music."

It was hard for him to imagine anybody who hated music, but he knew there had been complaints, so he was grateful for anything. "If you say an hour," he said, "then so be it."

"No, I think you're right," she said. "I think we'll switch it to an hour and a half, then see how that goes. I will schedule it for between four and five-thirty on Saturday afternoons, and then people could go for dinner afterward."

He nodded. "I'd really like that."

"Are you okay to play in the common room?" she asked. "Then we could make it a bit of a concert. I don't want to do it here in your room, where you'll clog up the hallway with people."

He laughed. "The common room works great," he said. "I can sit there in my wheelchair or maybe one of the chairs there," he said. "Honestly, I don't really know how strong I am or how long I can play."

"Well, it's a good time for a test then," she said, laughing. "We'll see you tomorrow." And, with that, she disappeared.

And he realized that today was Friday, which confirmed that tomorrow was Saturday, so he really only had a little over twenty-four hours to plan and to prepare. He brought it up with Shane. "Maybe we could figure out," he asked him hesitantly, "what's the best chair for me to do a concert with?"

Shane looked at him in surprise and said, "You know what? That's a really good idea because it makes a huge difference on your core and your back, doesn't it?"

"How I sit determines how flexible I am and what I can play," he said. "I need this arm free, and I must have the ability to stretch this other arm all the way out," he said.

Shane said, "Let's grab your guitar, and we'll work on the different chairs to see which one is best for you."

"I'll get my guitar," he said, as he maneuvered back into the wheelchair.

"Good," Shane said. "Let's meet in the common room, and we'll see what's there to choose from too."

By the time he arrived with his guitar in the common room, Shane was looking around at the various chairs, frowning.

"They don't look so great, do they?" Lance asked.

"It doesn't look bad though," Shane said. "How about a stool?"

Lance studied the lower stool and tried it out. He could hook one leg on the bottom railing and could sit with his other leg all the way to the floor for balance. He shifted so that he was sitting upright on the stool and sat for a good five minutes and then winced. "It's a good idea in terms of guitar-playing," he said, "but it's not such a good idea in terms of my hips and back."

"That's what I was worried about," Shane said. He looked over at a big armchair and said, "The arms here are too high for you to play, aren't they?"

Lance looked at it and nodded.

"This pot chair here has the same problem." Nearby was an open chair with no arms on the side. "What about something like this?" Shane asked. "You can lean back and get a little support."

Lance looked at it and laughed. "Are you moving the cat first?"

Shane looked at the cat, smiled, and said, "This is Max. He's taken over the place, although he hasn't been here all that long. He's only got three legs, but nobody told him that he's any different." He reached down and scooped up the cat. Max stretched in his arms, completely trusting that Shane wouldn't dump him. Max gave a little bit of a meow and closed his eyes, relaxing into Shane's embrace.

Lance looked at the cat and shook his head. "Such innocence."

"It's all about trust," Shane said. "Sit over here and give this a try."

Once he sat down in that chair, Lance nodded. "This one is perfect."

"Then let's shift it," he said. 'Where would you like it to be so you can face everybody?"

Looking around, Lance shrugged and said, "Well, how about over there in that corner? Then, as people come in, they can sit wherever they want."

So, they set that up, and Lance sat there a bit. He really wanted to strum the strings, but he didn't want to break Dani's trust that he wouldn't play indoors except on scheduled times. But he could run his hands up and down the strings, pretending like he was playing to test out his back. The chair was small enough that he could spread his legs on the corner and push his back right up against the chair for support. He smiled up at Shane. "You know what? This might work."

"Good," Shane said, and they talked about how to sit properly with his back getting the support he needed so that he wasn't completely exhausted at the end of his concert.

Just then a man walked up and went straight to the piano. They watched in fascination as he opened it right up.

Shane asked, "Are you supposed to be working on that?"

The man, surprised to hear somebody talking to him, turned, looked at the two men, and said, "Oh, hi. Yeah, I'm here to tune it. Sounds like somebody here wants to play it, so they hired me to get it fixed. Looks like it's been a while."

Lance could feel something really bloom inside him. "Did Dani do that for me?" he asked Shane.

Shane slid him a sideways look. "Everybody here cares about your recovery," he said. "It's a simple-enough thing to do, and, yes, it sounds very much like her," he said, laughing. "So, enjoy. I don't know when it'll be ready for you to play, and I doubt you can just sit down and run off a few songs, but it's something for you to consider. Maybe next weekend?"

Lance really wanted to walk over there and place his fingers on the ivories. It had been years since he'd played the piano, and it had always been one of the best mediums for him. It was a completely different kind of instrument from the guitar and even the trumpet. He loved them all, but, at the same time, something was just so special about playing a piano. As it was, his session with Shane was almost over, and it was hard to leave, but, as he wheeled away from the piano tuner, he turned and asked him, "When will you be done with that?"

"I'll be a good couple hours here yet," he said, "but definitely by the end of day."

"Perfect, thanks," he said. He looked up at Shane. "I guess Dani would know if it's me, wouldn't she?"

"Most likely, if you're any good, yes," he said, laughing. "But you can bet this may flush out a few other guys who want to sit down and pound on the keys. And some of them may be good too."

"That would be amazing," he said. "I love sitting down and playing impromptu sessions," he said, "just jamming with a few friends. There's nothing like it."

"Sounds like my version, minus the musical instruments and your talent, with a couple guys hanging around the barbecue with a couple beers," he said.

"Almost," he said, "I've had lots of friends over the years who played, but I don't know anybody right now who does."

"That's okay," Shane said, "maybe you'll meet one or two here."

Chapter 11

AS IT NEARED four o'clock, Jessica got nervous. Maybe she shouldn't have started this. Maybe he wasn't ready. Maybe she was pushing him? She didn't know why she was so nervous, but she was. She walked into the cafeteria to see Dennis handing out ice cream cones again. She looked at him and said, "You know that it wouldn't be so hard to keep the weight down if you would stop feeding us so well."

He laughed. "There's no such thing," he said. "If you just added a little exercise or walked a little more," he said, "you could afford a few hundred more calories."

"The trouble is," she said, in a low whisper, as she accepted the ice cream cone, "a hundred calories is a cookie. Something as delectable as this," she said, as she held up the cone, "has got to be more like five or six hundred calories."

He grinned. "A little less, but yeah," he replied.

She rolled her eyes at him. "As if I could resist ice cream. I've been trying to stick to veggies and protein as it is," she said.

"Well, whatever you're doing, it's working," he said. "I haven't seen you gain an ounce since you got here. Of course, you've also been working at a dead run day in and day out too."

"Well, there's that. But most of us staffers are aware of how easy it would be to pack on the pounds, courtesy of your kitchen, so we're extra mindful," she said with a laugh. Taking her ice cream, she walked back to the common area and realized a few of the chairs had been rearranged to not only allow for wheelchairs to come in but also for people to sit and just listen. And the piano was open and had been polished. She walked over and ran her fingers over the beautiful white keys. They made a lovely set of scales, but she had absolutely no idea how to play. Wouldn't it be nice if she did?

She sat down on the piano bench, facing the room, and enjoyed her ice cream cone. A few people arrived at about a quarter to four, and she wasn't sure if they were coming for the concert or if they were just coming because it was the common room and available when they wanted to be away from their rooms. She understood that very well.

By the time the scheduled concert hour neared, her ice cream was gone, and she'd slipped out and picked up coffee. She was seated once more on the piano bench, when she watched Lance roll his wheelchair to the front, then carefully shift over to the chair he had picked to use for today. He had the guitar with him, he looked over at her with a smile and said, "Well, I guess it's time, isn't it?"

She nodded. "A few people are already here for you," she said encouragingly.

He shook his head. "I'm playing for myself," he said. "People will come and like it, or they won't. I just want the time to play."

Slipping the guitar pick over his finger, he quickly thrummed the chords, then immediately launched into a country song and then slipped into a feel-good song, then sad, and back over to happy. She lost track as he took them through this emotional river. By the time he drifted off the last note from his guitar, an hour had passed. As soon as silence filled the room, she looked around to see that it was completely full of people. Once they realized he was done, they clapped like crazy. He looked up, surprised to see so many people here and gave a lazy smile.

She hopped to her feet and said, "That was absolutely superb," and clapped even harder. He shrugged. Dani was here too.

"I did say that you could go for another half hour," she said, "but, if you're tired, don't overdo it," she warned Lance.

He shook out his arms and said, "Actually, if you guys have a little bit of tolerance," he said, "I'd love to try out that piano."

Dani looked at Jessica in surprise and then nodded. "Don't you need some time to practice first though?"

"I don't know," he said. "Let's see." And, with that, he sat down beside Jessica, smiled at her, and his fingers spread out over the keys. Closing his eyes, he immediately jumped into Beethoven's Fifth Symphony. There were gasps of shock as the music thundered through the room.

Although it may have hurt him, he gave absolutely no sign of it. He ripped into song after song after song, but Jessica could see the strain starting to set in.

After twenty-five minutes, she reached out a gentle hand and touched his shoulder. He tilted his head against her hand ever-so-lightly, and moved into a very slow serenade. By the time he got through the song, she could see that he was done. He dropped his hands to his lap and turned to face everyone. "Looks like my time is up. Thank you all so much for listening. That will be all for tonight."

With that, the crowd erupted into a thunderous applause. She looked around and realized at least seventy-five people were here, although there could have been twice that many; she had no way of knowing because they were so jammed in the room. Somewhere off to the side was Shane. She walked through half the crowd that was slowly dissipating, noticing that the other half rushed to crush around Lance. She joined Shane and said, "That was freaking unbelievable."

Shane nodded, visibly impressed. "He told me that he was a musician, but I didn't realize how much of a musician. He's the real deal," he said. "As I sat back here and watched him, it was clear to me just how much we really have to do."

"My God, the piano, he really killed it!"

"He did, and that's a whole other can of worms to work on," he said. "I don't know if you noticed, but he didn't use his other foot for the pedals."

"I didn't notice at all," she said. "Please don't tell me that, instead of enjoying that wonderful music, you spent the whole time working, designing changes to his program?" She turned to look back at Lance, but he was completely surrounded by people. "He is beyond talented," she said, still in awe.

"Concert level," Shane said, crossing his arms over his chest. "I wonder why he didn't go into that full-time."

She shook her head. "That's a question we need to get to the bottom of," she said. "And, if this is what he wants to do for his future," she said, "maybe it's time to pursue his gift. Do you think it's possible to get him to the point where he's capable of doing this for more than an hour and a half?"

"Most concerts are about ninety minutes," he said.

"Concerts, yes," she said gently, "but not necessarily practice."

"Good point," he said. "An hour and a half a day probably isn't enough, is it?"

"I'd bet he'd play all day if he could, but I have no idea really. As far as practice goes though, I don't think he wants to tour and do concerts at that level," she said.

"But a bar in town, that's a whole different story," Shane said, clearly still focused, his mind spinning with the details of the challenge before them.

She smiled. "So, let's see if we can get him to that point," she said.

"I talked to him about a couple live-music bars in town, but I don't think he's done anything about it."

"I've gone to one a couple times," she said. "I wonder if I could talk to them myself."

She pondered that, while Shane leaned closer and said, "If you do, don't let him know you're doing it. It's one thing to think that other people are helping. It's another thing to have them doing things because they think you can't."

"That's not why I would do it," she protested. "I just happen to get into town a little easier than he can."

"I know," he said, "but pride is a touchy thing."

She rolled her eyes at him. "Particularly with the male species."

He burst out laughing.

When she looked over at Lance, he was watching the two of them, frowning. She gave him a bright smile and then walked over. "Are you ready to go for dinner?" she asked.

"Yeah, I am kind of tired now and hungry. Starving, actually." Several of the others crowded around them, and one of them said, "Let's go. We can all have dinner together."

She loved that camaraderie, that sense of inclusion. He

really needed that. It was acceptance at his peer level, and that was so important. She stepped back as they headed toward the cafeteria.

Shane motioned and said, "Are you letting him go alone?"

"I don't know," she said, shoving her hands into her pockets. "This is important for him too," she said. "He has a chance to make some friends here."

"No reason he can't make friends with you there," he said, giving her a gentle nudge. "Go join them, and you'll be accepted as part of it all as well."

She frowned, hesitating and hating that part of her which said she didn't belong, but Shane wasn't having it.

"Go," he said. She shot him a look, and he just shook his head. "Don't even begin to give me excuses," he said. "This is your one chance to join him, as if you were at a dinner party. Get out there and go. Let your own light shine a little bit too."

"My light doesn't shine very bright," she said with a half laugh.

"That's because you don't let it," he said. "Lately you've been all about getting Lance to shine," he said. "Now you're feeling like you don't think you're good enough or something, which is crazy," he said, shaking his head.

She considered it, shrugged, and then said, "Okay, but if it doesn't work out—"

"If it doesn't work out," he said in a sarcastic voice, "you'll try again tomorrow."

LANCE GLANCED AROUND, but he was surrounded by other

patients, and they were all talking and laughing about concerts they'd been to. One of them used to jam on the drums, and another used to play trumpet. He was really happy that his music had sparked something for a lot of them. The energy was high and the conversation light and bubbly. Yet something was missing. He kept looking around, but he saw no sign of Jessica.

Finally a hand gently touched his shoulder, and he recognized it immediately. He also sensed something settling inside him at her arrival. He reached up a hand, grabbed hers, and tried to push his wheelchair with just his free hand, which didn't work so well. She chuckled, squeezed his fingers, and, grabbing his wheelchair, pushed him from behind. He thought about arguing, then shrugged and gave up. The truth of matter was, his arms were sore, and he was tired. And he was also grateful to have her here with him. As they got to the cafeteria, Dennis waited for them behind the counter. He looked up and beamed.

"There you are, Jessica," he said. "I wondered where you got off to, and then, when I heard the music, I figured, when it came to an end, you'd be all rushing down to eat." Next he looked at Lance and said, "I got to tell you, man, that was some of the best music I've heard in a long time."

That comment set everybody else off too. Lance felt warm inside, in a way he hadn't in a very long time. He wasn't sure who had brought it up, but it was all about acceptance, finding your place, and being true to who you were. A guy stepped back and, "Let Lance go first tonight."

Looking around, Lance said, "Hey, you don't need to give me any special privileges," he said. "I'm just the same as you guys."

Jessica plunked a tray into his lap, and she said, "Absolutely you are, and everybody else here has their own specialties too," she said. "But tonight, you made us all very, very happy because that music was like nectar from the gods."

A round of clapping came at her words. Lance just laughed.

Dennis said, "Okay, then. What can I get for the man of the hour? It's steak night, by the way."

Feeling like a celebrity and a bit of a fool, he said, "Actually I'd love a steak."

Dennis's eyebrows shot up, and he said, "Medium rare, rare?"

"Medium rare, baked potato, and a Caesar salad on the side."

Dennis nodded. "You got it. Anybody else?"

Immediately half the gang behind him chimed in.

"Guess we'll have to have steak night more often," Dennis said.

"It's the whole dinner-and-a-show feeling," Jessica said.

"You may have something there. Anyway, where will you all sit? I'll start bringing out plates as they come up."

Chapter 12

THEY HEADED FOR the deck in the open air. It was still a hot afternoon, though it was overcast today, so it wasn't like they were sitting in the direct sun. They collected their drinks, and, as a group, they all headed out to the deck and pulled chairs and tables together, so they could all sit somewhat close together. They ended up in a big square, with some seated inside and some out. Laughing and joking, Jessica hadn't felt this good or this much a part of something since she'd arrived. As she realized that, she was also aware that this was really important. And the whole time Lance stayed beside her, being part of it all.

He reached over and gripped her fingers. "Thank you."

"I didn't do anything," she said, her lips kicking up in the corners.

"Yes, you did," he said. "You helped set this up, and you stayed with me the whole time."

She looked at him in surprise. "That matters?"

"It matters," he said. "I'm not exactly sure how or why, but I'm glad that you were there to share this with me."

She squeezed his fingers back and whispered, "I am too."

Just then Dennis came over with a great big tray. "I've got steaks here," he said. "Put up your hands so I can remember who ordered what," he said, in a cheerful voice. In no time he had those plates distributed, and Lance had a big slab of steak, a baked potato, and Caesar salad in front of him.

"Now this is awesome," he whispered.

Just when they thought dinner couldn't get any better, Dennis came around with a few beers and some sparkling juice and said, "This is a night we all need to celebrate," he said. "It's nonalcoholic beer, since most everybody is on medications, but let's make the most of it."

Everybody raised a can and cheered.

Just something was so special about this evening. It had started with Lance's music, but it had also stretched into dinner. She was on the inside of the big square they had created, as were another twenty-odd guys, with another forty or so on the outside. It was freaking awesome. Dennis was working like a madman, trying to keep them all happy.

She called out to him and said, "Dennis, cheers to you for making this happen." He stopped, looked at her as a big smile split his face, and he said, "Cheers to you for your part in it too."

She laughed. "Okay, this mutual admiration society," she said, "we're both members."

He howled with laughter at that. Then he said, "Well, when you guys are all done, I've got fresh raspberry cheese-cake coming out too."

They all just moaned in joy and tucked into their meals. She was having a steak too, but hers was about half the size of Lance's, and her salad was twice the size of his. She skipped the baked potato, and, of course, Dennis had remembered. It had been more than perfect.

THE WHOLE EVENING produced a glow that lasted for days. Lance went back to play the piano for a few minutes at a time, trying to adjust his spine on the bench, wondering if he could do it long-term. Shane was working on strengthening his ability to sit on something hard like that. He could get a cushion, but it wasn't the same thing. It was more the angle, where he had to sit with his back straight, yet get his arms spread out and his fingers as wide as they needed to go.

It was the leaning forward and the pulling back again that was absolutely killing his system. Shane had devised some very specific exercises to allow Lance to do it a whole lot easier. He paid in a big way for that concert and had ended up in the hot tub before going to bed, just to ease up on the cramps. Shane had even given him some muscle relaxants to hopefully stop the muscle knots.

But unfortunately he'd woken up early in the morning, nearly screaming in pain from muscle cramps anyway. The night nurse had come and had helped massage some of them down, had given him some more medication, but the news had gotten back to Shane first thing in the morning, and he was all over it. He also had Lance on some vitamins— calcium, magnesium, and a few other things that he didn't recognize—in order to help calm down the muscles.

"When you overwork them," Shane said, "they'll spasm like that."

"Well, I really hope not to go through that again," he said. "It was painful."

"I know it is," he said. "It's a movement we haven't worked on at all."

"We were doing so much," he said, "and I didn't tell you that the leg was really struggling too."

"You didn't have to," he said. "I was at the concert and

watched," he said. "I could tell by the way you were moving what some of the issues were."

"Yeah," he said. "I keep hoping."

"And don't *just* worry," he said. "You keep planning for success. You know what they say. If you fail to plan, you plan to fail."

At that moment, Lance stopped and stared at him. "Wow," he said. "I don't think I've ever heard that before."

"You should have, and, if you haven't, it's something you need to emblazon in your brain," Shane said. "Some things in life you have to take concrete steps toward in order to make them happen. If you want to get back to playing like you were," he said, "then we need to strengthen some of these muscles, but we can't do it and cause a problem with some others. So it's got to be a full-body thing."

"So, what are you thinking? Will I get there?" He lay on his back, exhausted from the exercises he'd been doing with Shane and his knees.

"Absolutely," Shane replied. "Not only will we get you back there but we'll get you better than ever," he said. "That's my motto."

"If you say so," Lance said, and he groaned. "I really would like to get into that pool and do some weightless water exercises," he said.

"Good idea," he said. "That's a full-body workout too. How about we do that this afternoon? Meet you down there at what? Two o'clock? Or do you have any other appointments this afternoon?"

"Not today," he said. "Two o'clock it is."

By the time two o'clock rolled around, Lance wasn't sure he should have signed up for anything more. Most days, Shane just wiped him out, and now he'd added in swimming. But, even though Lance was exhausted and in pain, he was also looking forward to it in a big way. He also wanted to make sure he got some sleep tonight, and, if this is what it would take, then that was fine. At the pool, he rolled up to the side to see Shane standing there, waiting for him.

He assessed the wheelchair and the look on Lance's face. "Starting next week," he said, "we'll get you up on crutches. You're using the wheelchair as an extension of yourself."

Lance looked up at him, frowned, and said, "It is an extension of myself."

"It is," he said, "but, at some point, it can also become a crutch. And, for that to stop, you have to have crutches."

"So, I get rid of one crutch and end up with two?" he asked sarcastically.

Shane's smile was bright and flashy, showing his white teeth. "Okay, funny guy, into the water with you."

Putting down the locks on his wheelchair, Lance slowly stood, hobbled the few steps to the railing, and, rather than making any attempt at a bit of form, he just fell into the water. When the warm water closed over him, and his body floated midpool, something was just so freeing and glorious about it. He slowly rose to the surface, brushed the water out of his eyes, and smiled up at Shane. "What is there about being in the water that is so awesome?"

"Well, nothing in your body has to work as hard to be there," he said, "so it's very freeing. So you can swim?"

"Fine time to ask that," Lance said with a laugh. "I used to swim very well, but now I don't know."

"Try a couple laps, so I can take a look," Shane said.

Lance dove under the water, came up to the surface, and started with a strong right crawl. He flipped and turned at the other end, came back, then flipped, and turned again. He did this a couple more times until he could feel his body fatiguing. He came up halfway in the middle and then slowly floated toward the shallow end.

Shane was making notes.

"So, is it good news or bad news?" Lance asked.

"I'd say it's great news," Shane said. "We have some work to do, but you're doing quite well."

"It feels great," he said.

"Yep, and you were strong enough to do six laps today, even after a workout," he said. "So we'll need to work you up to twenty laps," he said, as he continued to write notes.

Lance lay in the water and just floated. "Something is so special about this," he murmured. "Dani was so right to put in this pool."

"She did it quite early on," Shane said. "We get the same reaction from everybody who comes here. The pool is an added benefit, and you're free to come here after we've gotten through a certain amount of training," he said. "There's no lifeguard on duty, and everybody has to understand that."

"Got it. What about the staff members?"

"Same thing. They're allowed to come and go after physiotherapy sessions are over," he said. "So you'll often find them down here Sundays, tanning or swimming in the pool or just sitting in the hot tub."

"That would be nice too," he said. Pulling himself up, he sat on one of the lower steps and asked, "Am I done for today?"

Shane looked at him and smiled. "Are you kidding? We haven't even gotten started," he said gently.

Lance winced. "Okay, then, do your worst."

Chapter 13

JESSICA HEARD ABOUT the swimming over the next couple days. Lance told her about it. Shane told her about it. And even a couple other people told her about it. In other words, everybody was excited that Lance's progress on land—which had been slow but steady—was nothing like his progress in the water. She was happy for him. The water was a full-body workout, and he would show quite a rapid improvement, if he kept it up. When she came in at lunchtime one afternoon, tired and stressed with some computer glitch going on, Dennis looked at her.

"Uh-oh."

She gave him a wan smile. "Honestly, it's not bad. Just computer stuff."

He gave a mock shudder. "I don't like computer stuff at all," he said. "So, what can I get you for lunch?"

"A chicken Caesar salad, please."

He quickly made her a beautiful Caesar salad, then chopped some chicken and put it on top for her. She smiled broadly and said, "You'll make some woman a great husband," she said with a laugh. "This is perfect." He just smiled at her and turned to the next customer in line. She wandered onto the deck but couldn't handle the direct sun at this time of day and stepped into the shade a bit.

"Hey, why don't you sit with me?" a man called out to

her.

She turned to see Lance. She walked over with a weary smile and sat down.

He looked at her and frowned.

"I'm fine," she said. "We've just got some real glitchy computer stuff going on right now, and it's frustrating me to no end."

He shook his head. "I love technology, but only when it works."

She laughed and laughed. "I think that's how we all feel," she said. "And all too often it doesn't work at all."

"True enough." He looked at her lunch and said, "Now that looks really good."

"I was hoping for something that would give me vitamins and nutrients but with a little protein at the same time, so I can destress and head back to work," she said. "So, how's the swimming going?"

"It's wonderful," he said. "I would go in every day, but Shane wants me to up some of my regular gym routines and to ease back on some of the water stuff."

"I'm sure it's more about balance than anything," she said.

"Absolutely," he said. "Still, it's frustrating because I'd rather do the water."

"Which is why you have to do the land," she said, laughing. He just grinned. She looked at his empty plate. "I guess you got here before I did."

"It's almost one-thirty," he said, checking his watch. "I have to go for one of my doctor visits and then another at two-thirty."

"Wow," she said. "I forgot your schedule is always so busy here."

"It's seriously busy," he said. "I never expected that."

"A lot of different avenues to improve," she said.

He nodded. "True enough, but my first appointment is with the medical doctor to go over my meds, my supplements, and my general physical condition," he said.

"That's very important," she said. "Better not miss that one."

"I don't dare miss any of them," he said. "I hated going to the shrink at first, but now, well"—he gave a light shrug and a lopsided grin—"I am finding it to be very helpful."

She beamed. "Good," she said, "because, like I'm sure he said, it's all about balance. Emotional, spiritual, and physical."

"I don't know about the spiritual part," he said, "but the emotional and the mental are finally coming into line."

"You're doing so great. It's really amazing," she said, leaning in with a smile.

He reached across and covered her hand with his. "Thank you."

She shrugged and settled back a little bit, but she was pleased. "Are we getting another concert next weekend?"

He grinned boyishly. "Dani did ask me about that," he said. "A lot of the other patients were hoping that it could be a regular thing."

She stared at him in delight. "What about the dissenters?"

"Well, apparently they've been fairly quiet this time. Maybe just having it as a scheduled occasion was enough to make the difference."

"It probably was," she said, "so it's good news all around."

"Exactly."

"So, is that a yes then?"

He shrugged. "I'll listen to Shane on this one," he said.

"And what does Shane say?"

"He said that I could do it again, but that he wants to change my seating."

"Oh, I like that idea," she said. "If he can sort out how you should be sitting, and you can find a way to make that work along with your natural playing style," she said, "that's probably all working together for the good of your core."

"Well, that's the thing," he said. "You're the first one to mention my natural playing style. Because really, when you get into playing, you don't think about how you're sitting," he said. "So it's a little awkward because Shane always wants me to consider my posture, and, once I'm into the music, I don't think of anything but the music."

"So, go around the place and see if any other chairs would work for you," she said.

"Shane suggested that as well—or maybe even an office chair or something that will give me a little bit better lower-back support."

She nodded thoughtfully. "We have a bunch of chairs in the offices. You can always ask Dani about having one for the concert."

"Yeah. Shane's got a whole pile of chairs for our next session that he wants to work with." At that, she stared at him, and he nodded. "They're all lined up—like fifteen of them."

She chuckled. "The thing about Shane is," she said, "if you put him on a mission, he'll see it through. And he'll see you through, to the best you can be. So, if he has all these chairs lined up to figure out how to make it work for you," she said, "I'd let him do it."

"I'm not sure I have a choice," Lance said, laughing. "Shane is beyond determined."

"And so are you," she said gently. "And you should be. You're very talented, and, if this is what you want for your second career, then go for it."

"I never thought I could have a career at it," he said, "and I still don't know that." He stared off in the distance. "Shane mentioned a couple bars in town."

"And would that be where you might want to play?"

"I'm not sure," he said. "Somebody else mentioned YouTube, but I wouldn't have a clue how to monetize something like that."

"That may be something where you have your own channel to increase your visibility or something," she said. "I don't understand how that works either, but I'm sure it wouldn't take too much to figure it all out."

"Personally, I really enjoy the bar atmosphere," he said. "Especially a bar that plays jazz and the blues too."

"Well, like Shane said, a couple are in town. I've been to one of them," she said. "I know they have live music. I suppose I could always ask how they pick their musicians."

He looked at her, surprised, and then slowly nodded. "Well, whenever you're there next, if you wouldn't mind, it would be good information to have."

She smiled. "Absolutely," she said. "In fact, I'd be delighted. I really want you to succeed at this."

"What? Are you getting rid of me already?"

She gave him a slow smile and said, "Honestly, I'm trying to keep you close. If you find jobs in Dallas that you actually love and want to stay with," she said, "then maybe I'll be lucky, and you'll stay nearby when you're done with your rehab."

He looked at her in surprise, and then the most beautiful of smiles flashed across his face. "You know something? That's exactly what I was thinking too."

LANCE SHOULDN'T HAVE said anything to her about the clubs. That was putting a job on her shoulders that didn't belong there. If he couldn't go to the club and talk to the owners himself, he certainly shouldn't be the one playing there.

He'd always been independent.

This was on the edge of not.

He frowned at that. He hadn't had any qualms when he'd asked her initially, so what was the hindsight issue now? It's not like she'd shown any hesitation. Still, it worried him until Shane stopped him at his next session.

"What's going on?"

"Just pondering the fine line between dependence and independence."

Shane gave a low whistle. "Now that's an interesting argument. I think the difference is in the ability to accept help when needed, versus using help when it's not needed. Everyone needs help sometime. It's abusing that help that makes the difference."

"So, dependence should be acknowledged when one has no choice, and independence should be exercised if one can make that choice."

Shane looked at him in surprise. "If that pertains to the situation at hand, yes. But remember. It's also a gift to ask for or to accept a little help. As long as you don't abuse it, it's all good." With that, Shane motioned at the medicine ball.

"Now let's get back at it."

Lance laughed and bent from the knees to pick it up. He'd just wait and see. If he'd crossed a line with her, hopefully she would tell him. And, in the future, he'd have to remember not to ask for something if he could do it himself.

His future was at stake here.

Chapter 14

J ESSICA COULDN'T STOP thinking about the clubs in
town. As soon as she was done with work today, she
skipped dinner and headed into town, where she stopped off
at the first of two clubs. It was open but not with any live
music at the moment. It didn't really get busy until around
seven p.m. She walked to the manager's office and knocked.
Surprised, somebody from the inside called out to come in.
She pushed open the door, then smiled and introduced
herself.

The manager looked at her and said, "What can I do for
you?"

"Hello, I'm a nurse from Hathaway House," she said.
"We have a veteran who's recovering after a lengthy series of
surgeries from service-related injuries," she said. "He's a
musician and a very talented one at that. He used to play at
jazz and blues clubs before he went into the service, and I'm
wondering how you run live music at your club."

"Well, I have a lineup," he said. "We're always looking
for new talent, of course, but I really need somebody who
knows how to play the blues," he said, "not just any musician. That won't cut it around here."

"Got it," she said. "What I should have done was
brought you a tape of his music."

"Or, if he's the one interested in the work," the manager

said, "he should have come in person."

"Oh, of course," she said cheerfully. "But his rehab is pretty intensive right now, and I just wondered how the system even worked. Like, whether you paid them or if they live on tips alone, and how often, how long the sets are, and what nights he would play here."

He laughed. "In other words, you're checking it out for your friend. That's all cool," he said, "but, before I'd bring him in as a repeat performer," he said, "I'd want him up there on that stage, playing in person, before I offered him a chance at playing at night."

"Understood," she said with a smile.

Frowning, he tapped his pen on a pad of paper and said, "Like I said, I do have a couple regulars who play here a couple nights. But one of the guys I've got now is planning on leaving."

"When is he leaving?"

"I think at the end of next month," he said. "I've been trying to convince him to stay, but, for two nights a week, it's hardly enough to keep anybody's rent paid."

"I wanted to ask you about that," she said, settling into the visitor's chair. "Do you pay them?"

"I do, but it's for the evening," he said. "And I'm not telling you how much because that'll be between me and whoever."

"And what about tips?"

"The tips are his," he said. "Some nights you get a lot, and some nights you may not get any."

"He used to get hundreds, occasionally one thousand in tips."

At that, his brows rose. "He'd have to be real good for that."

"Oh, he's good," she said. "But, like I said, he's busy with rehab and currently still using a wheelchair, working on getting into crutches and hopefully walking."

"That'll always garner sympathy too," the manager said.

"And that's not something he wants," she said. "Pride is a hard thing for a guy like him."

"Well, if and when he gets there," he said, "he is welcome to come by and show me what he can do."

"That's great. Thank you." She hopped her feet and said, "Do you happen to have a card?"

He handed her a card, and, as she walked to the door, he asked, "You sure he's any good?"

"I think so, but come and see for yourself," she said. "He's playing between four and five-thirty on Saturday afternoons at Hathaway House," she said. "We can't have him playing all the time because some residents object to the noise," she said.

He just rolled his eyes at that. "Always one in every crowd, isn't there?" he murmured.

"Indeed," she said, "but, nonetheless, for the next couple Saturdays he'll be playing before dinnertime at Hathaway House."

"We'll see," he said and gave her a dismissive wave.

She took the hint and headed into the main room again. She checked out the area and noted it had a very nice simple stage with lots of seating. She'd been here in the evenings, when the place was standing room only, and remembered that she had really enjoyed the live music. She didn't remember how long it lasted, but she thought it may have been well past an hour and a half, so that was a concern. But, then again, Lance didn't have to necessarily play the whole evening. She was about to turn and ask the manager if he ever used multiple entertainers in one evening, when the bartender asked her if she needed anything.

She headed to him and said, "I was wondering about the live music," she said. "Do you ever have more than one player in an evening?"

He nodded. "All the time. Everybody's got their own style, and not everybody wants to play for hours on end," he said. "Usually three hours is max for a gig for one," he said. "Sometimes we're open until one or two o'clock in the morning," he said, "so it depends."

"Got it," she said. "That probably explains why the manager didn't want to talk about money and how much he'd pay someone to be here. It's not comparing apples to apples."

"He's fair, and they do fine," he said, "and they do well on tips too."

"Yeah, but what are we talking about—a hundred or two?"

"I'd say seven or eight hundred. I've seen some of the guys in here break a couple thousand, and then we have some who are only so-so, and they'll get a couple hundred," he said. "And, if it's a bad night and a big game is on the TV, nobody will be here, and you'll be lucky if you get any tips at all."

"So, nothing you can really count on."

He laughed. "No, nothing you can count on. But, if you're any good, you'll have a following, and everybody will show up each Friday and Saturday night like clockwork."

"Got it," she said, and, with a smile of thanks, she headed to the second bar, not liking it quite as much. But, with the same information, more or less, she headed back to Hathaway House, sneaking in just in time to grab dinner before the kitchen closed.

Dennis looked at her, surprised. "Where did you sneak off to?"

"I had to run into town," she said easily, as she reached for a big chicken breast and steamed veggies. "As usual this looks wonderful."

"It is," he said, "because Ilse sets up that menu, and she won't let anybody do anything less than a great job."

"We see a lot more of her outside of her kitchen too," she said, "now that Keith's here."

"Nothing quite like it," Dennis said. "Look at you. You're way more involved than you used to be too."

"I'm not sure that's a good thing," she said with a laugh.

"Maybe, but it keeps you more alive," he muttered.

"Sure enough." She smiled and took her plate outside. She was definitely hungry, and now she didn't know what she should say to Lance because he couldn't do live performances weekly for quite a while. He certainly wouldn't want to play in the wheelchair, but maybe he could do it partly in a chair and partly in a wheelchair. But that pride of his. She could understand it though, because she wasn't sure she would be any different if she was in the same physical shape.

Keeping her thoughts to herself, she went through the next few days until he finally noticed and asked, "What are you so pensive about?"

"Not a whole lot," she said. "I went in and talked to the two clubs in town."

He stopped and stared at her. "Wow," he said. "You do remember the fact that I probably won't be ready for a couple months, right?"

"You also said I could," she reminded him.

He nodded. "But I don't want to feel pressured or

pushed into it," he said. "I'm not sure when I'll be ready."

She settled back and nodded slowly. "Of course not," she replied, "but you did say that I could talk to them."

Feeling irritable and obviously not quite ready to make that kind of decision, he nodded but left soon afterward.

She sat here, drinking her coffee, wondering if she had been just too eager on his behalf. It was a fault of hers that she had encountered before. She tended to see a way forward, and then she would jump at it, getting things to move in the direction she thought they should. But maybe she hadn't listened to him enough. Maybe she had done this because she wanted to see him do well, without considering if he was ready to, yet. And, even if he was ready to do well, that didn't mean he was ready to go in that direction. She groaned, trying to remember the original conversation but struggling.

"Sounds like you mucked it up again," she said irritably to herself. And, for the next couple days, she and Lance kind of danced around each other, both ignoring this particular conversation. When it came time for his Saturday four o'clock performance, she made sure she was there to listen to the music. She also searched to see if the bar guy was here, but she saw no sign of him. Disappointed, though she really didn't know why, she sat back and just listened to the music. The crowd was just as riotous as last time, if not even more enthusiastic.

This time, instead of going to dinner with him, she stepped outside and just sat on the deck at her own table. The music still throbbed through her veins, and it felt wonderful. He was very talented, with a gift that he should share with the world. A world that would be blessed to receive it. But somehow he had to both get strong enough to do it and then actually want to do it, which was a whole different story. She'd met all kinds of people who had the talent to do something but just weren't interested in doing it.

Like going to school with all the top brainiacs, and one was a girl who Jessica knew belonged to the Mensa group. Her IQ was just off the wall. But all she wanted to do was nails, and she became a salon manicurist.

At the time Jessica had been horrified, but the woman looked at her and said, "That's just your perception. If you didn't know I was in Mensa, then you wouldn't care," she said. "So now you're judging me for not doing what you think I should do."

That had stuck with Jessica throughout the years. As she sat here, in the peace and quiet, listening to all the boisterous activity behind her, she was quietly happy.

When Lance reached out to her twenty minutes later, he said, "There's ice cream, if you want one?"

She turned to look at him in surprise. He had a big ice cream cone in his hand. She laughed. "I ate plenty of dinner," she said. "No room for more."

"You didn't join me for dinner. How come?"

"Oh," she said, "you looked like you were doing just fine."

"Is that the only time you come looking for me?" he asked curiously. "When you think I need a friend?"

"Not at all," she said, getting a little defensive. "I just thought tonight I'd like some time alone, and you had lots of friends around you, and you looked to be happy."

"I can be happy and alone, and I can be happy and have friends," he said. "It was nice tonight, and they all seem to appreciate the music. But they didn't seem to appreciate me before the music, so it feels weird."

She chuckled. "I can see that, but I don't think we can blame them too much. People often don't know what they want or like until they hear it, and then they're quite surprised at how much they enjoyed it."

"Maybe," he said.

Then she realized that he'd traded the wheelchair for crutches. She slowly dropped her legs from the railing and turned to face him. "How is that going?" she said mildly, a head nod at his crutches.

"Slowly," he said, reaching for a chair and sitting down a little hard. "Very slowly."

"Any progress is good though," she said.

"Maybe," he said, "but, at the same time, it's change, and I guess I haven't been all that comfortable with change."

"I think you've done really well since you've arrived," she said impulsively.

He burst out laughing. "Like I said before, you're a great cheerleader."

"That doesn't mean I don't mean what I say," she said, "because I do."

"I'm glad to hear that," he said with a chuckle, "because it's nice to know that you've always got my back."

"And apparently," she said, "I'm guilty of pushing you, and, for that, I'm sorry."

"You mean, the blues club?" He shook his head. "I told you that it was okay to talk to them."

"But when I did, you weren't happy."

"It's that whole *change* thing again," he said. "It took me a few days to figure it out, but apparently I don't like change in any form," he said. "It came up with Shane too. He says that every time he changes my routine, I protest for one reason or another, but it comes down to the issue of change."

"Of course. When he makes a change in your routine, you have to work different muscles," she said. "So I'm not sure I'd like that myself."

"Oh, come on. You embrace new things," he said, "and that makes a huge difference."

"Maybe," she said, "but I'm more the eager beaver. You point me in a direction, and I'll tear forward to see how far we can go. Unfortunately I'm frequently halfway there before I even give a thought to the prudence of going there in the first place."

"Whereas, I'm more the plodding tortoise, who can see a path coming up ahead. And it's a good thing that I can see it, so I have time to prepare for it before I ever get there," he said, in a wry tone, laughing at himself.

"I think there is room in the world for both of us," she said. "There's no competition, and there's no race."

"No," he said, "and that's a good thing because, since I got here, I've not been in a racing spirit," he said. "So it's a really good thing there wasn't actually one to worry about."

"It's just a matter of accepting where you're at," she said, "and accepting that you're different and that everybody else around you is different too."

"We're back to that cheerleader again," he said, and they sat in companionable silence while he ate his ice cream.

She looked at it again and said, "Now that you're done," she said, "I want one."

He laughed. "I could go for a second one myself." She stared at him in astonishment. He shrugged. "What? I'm just a growing boy, you know."

She snorted at that and said, "Hang on. I'll go see if Dennis is still around." As she headed back into the kitchen, he saw her coming, looked at her suspiciously, and said, "Are you trying to rob me of my ice cream again?" He spoke in a mock horrified voice.

"Yep," she said, "two, please, as Lance thinks he can go for a second one."

"Boy, since that kid started to eat, it's like every day he gains more and more of an appetite," Dennis said, as he busily scooped up ice cream for them. When he handed her two big cones, she grinned a big fat smile and said, "Dennis, these look delicious. You are a master."

"Yeah, well, remember, I'm not to blame for any changes to your waistline," he said with a laugh, reminding her of their previous conversation.

"I've been so busy lately," she said, "I think I've lost weight." Off again, she headed back out to the deck.

As soon as he got his hands on his second ice cream cone, Lance smacked his lips and said, "Wow. You know there's a lot to be said about this place."

"It seems to be a good place for you," she said.

"Now that you guys have given me my music back," he said, "it's a great place for me."

AND LANCE MEANT it. Having that part of his world opened up again had filled him with so much soul satisfaction that he couldn't believe it. He remembered all the reasons why he hadn't even tried to handle musical instruments before, and he knew that he hadn't been at a stage of recovery where it was possible. But now it was possible, and he felt so blessed.

He wished he could play on the piano for a couple hours, just to work on that, but he wasn't sure if that would be asking too much. He was very grateful for the hour and a half he had every Saturday, but it was just that much harder to ask for more when people were already being so generous. He did bring it up with Shane on Monday morning.

"I don't know if we can move it to another location or not," Shane said. "I know it's on wheels but—"

"Right. It's in a very public location right now," Lance said. "Which means, if anybody else wanted to sit down and play, they can't."

"Nobody has, as far as I'm aware," Shane said, "but it's a good point."

Monday passed; Tuesday passed. And, by Wednesday, Lance couldn't resist. He crutched his way to the piano, shifted onto the bench, and just ran a few chords. Within a few minutes he pounded away at the keys. It was all he could do to force himself to stop after a couple songs, but he did and then managed to get his wheelchair and left. But just that much playing had the energy thrumming through his veins and a smile on his face.

Dani saw him later that day, and she asked, "Was that you on the keyboard?"

"Yes," he said. "Should I apologize? I just couldn't resist. I wanted to touch the music so badly that I couldn't stop myself."

"I didn't hear any complaints," she said with a smile, "so it's a case of making sure it's not too much."

He nodded. "It's nice to know that I could maybe play a couple songs and not hurt anybody's sense of propriety in this."

"People will be people," she said. "The guitar is at least mobile, and you can take it outside. But the piano? That's a different story."

"But you got it tuned," he said, "so we don't want to

waste it."

She chuckled. "No, we definitely don't want to waste that."

By the next Saturday he had already worked out a series of songs in his mind. Most were on his guitar, but then he would flip over to the piano and play a bit. By the time he was done this Saturday night, he didn't even want to stop. There were several cries for encores, and he played a couple, but, ever mindful of Dani's generosity, he had to shut it down, even though he had only exceeded his time by five minutes.

He thanked everybody for coming. "Listen. I'd play longer," he said, "but I'm grateful for the ninety-minute window we have right now and don't want to disrespect the privilege." The crowd agreed, but there were lots of groans and complaints. He smiled and said, "Hey, you know who to take it up with." They all enjoyed a laugh.

From the back, Dani said, "Hey, thanks for that, Lance. You just threw me under the bus."

He chuckled and said, "No, I definitely don't want to do that," he said. "Because of Dani, I can be here and can play at all."

That was the pattern for the next couple weeks, and he could feel himself building in strength—with Shane working on his back, his thighs, his posture, and even the way Lance held his neck. Sometimes they practiced with the guitar in his hand, and Shane would correct his posture to strengthen it, so Lance would be okay to play longer. Then they did the same thing on the piano.

"Too bad I don't have drums," he said. "I could really see myself pounding out some of that music."

"I imagine you are great as a drummer too," Shane said.

"Yes," he said, "I am. You'll be happy to know the positioning is different yet again."

"We'll get there," he said. "Maybe we'll take you to a music store in town, so I can have you sit on everything they offer, and I can take photos to study later."

Lance looked at him in surprise. "Wow," he said. "Actually, for drums, it would just be a stool," he said. "I used to sit on a round stool." Then he looked around the gym and pointed out one of the stools up against a desk. Something like that. Grabbing his crutches, he made his way over to the side and pulled the stool into the middle of the gym. Then, with his hands holding imaginary wooden drum sticks, he rapped on an imaginary set of drums. Shane watched carefully. When Lance finally stopped and looked over at Shane, Lance smiled sheepishly and said, "That was probably a pretty crazy-looking show."

"But I've got it on video," Shane said, "and it's very helpful to see how you're using your back." He played it so Lance could see the way he curved and bent.

"So, right across my shoulder blades, I've still got that curve that I'm supposed to be straightening up," he said. "It was really helpful to see it like that though."

"Exactly," Shane said. "You've come a long way. We're just tuning little bits and pieces now."

"Does that mean I'll get out of here soon?"

"Probably another eight to ten weeks," Shane said. "I don't want you to leave until you're strong, capable, and vibrant, and when you have a plan in place for moving forward," he said. "Too often people get impatient, and they leave because they have friends and family they want to get back to, or a career, and they're at that 80 percent mark," he said. "I want to get everybody to the 100 percent mark, so they can maintain what they've accomplished. There'll be some slippage," he said. "That's to be expected because you won't be having therapy every day. So you'll want to make sure you're at 100 percent, so the slippage only takes you back down to 90 or 95."

"Or I don't leave until I'm 120 percent," he said with a big smile. "And then I'm only at 100 when I'm done slipping."

"Or you don't slip at all," Shane said. "That's an option too."

They just chuckled and kept on working. Lance hadn't heard any more about the blues club from either Jessica or Shane. And he wouldn't for another few weeks. And, when he did, it came in a surprising form.

Chapter 15

J ESSICA LOOKED AT the email, surprised. She looked over at Dani. "Are you sure this email is for me?"

"I'm not exactly sure who it's for," she said, "but I figured you would be the one to start with. It's from the blues club."

"But I didn't give him my email. I just said I was from Hathaway House."

"It's definitely for *their contact at Hathaway House*," she said, "and it says he was talking to somebody from here," tapping the screen with her finger. "So, that would be you."

Jessica sat down to read the rest of the message and smiled. "He had told me that one of his musicians was planning on leaving. Apparently that has happened, so now he's looking for a replacement. I'd been extremely supportive of the idea, but I didn't want to push Lance into it. I got the feeling he felt like I was pushing," she said, "so I backed off immediately."

"Well, this sounds like a great opportunity," Dani said. "I don't know where Lance's progress is at or whether he could make it into town to do a show," she said, "but it might be a good way to find out."

"Right," Jessica said. "Maybe he could even start by doing just an hour and a half on a Friday night," she said enthusiastically. Then she remembered the distance that had come between them last time over this same topic. "But again, that sounds like me pushing, and this may not be what he wants to do," she said.

"So just print this off and let him decide," Dani said.

"The other thing is, it could all be for naught," she said. "Because he wanted Lance to go in and audition for a spot, if he was interested. I'd mentioned that he plays here on Saturdays, but that doesn't mean he plays the blues."

"Right," she said. "Again, dump it in his hands and see what he'd like to do."

"Will do," she said. She printed off a copy and tucked it into her pocket. It was a couple days before she had it at a time where she felt it was right to share it with Lance. She pulled it from her uniform pocket and handed it to him one morning when she headed down for coffee.

"What's this?" he asked, sitting up in his bed and unfolding it. He looked at it in surprise. "Wow, this again."

"Only if you want to," she said. "I'm not pushing, but I did stop in that one time, and he remembered, and he sent this email."

"But that also means going in for an audition," he said, "and going in for a whole evening. I don't think I can do that."

"Well," she said, "I guess there are a few options though."

"Maybe," he said. "I don't know." He nodded, tucked the email back into its folded form, and laid it on top of his table beside his coffee cup.

She could feel a sense of disappointment but had to remind herself that he would make whatever choice he felt was right for him. She glanced at her watch. "I've got to go," she said. "The day has started." And she headed back to her office.

Throughout the day, she wondered if he'd come to any decision but chose not to mention it. Several days later he still hadn't mentioned it, and she tucked away her expectations and tried to just let him do him. When Saturday whirled around, the common area was even more jam-packed than usual.

She laughed as she stood beside him. "You know something? Dani'll need to set this up in a bigger area."

"I was thinking the cafeteria," he said. "Maybe next time."

"Maybe this time," she said, as the place swelled with even more people. She looked over as Dani neared and asked, "Can we move this to the cafeteria?"

She looked surprised and then nodded. "Let me check to see how many people are in there." She headed to the cafeteria and returned a few minutes later. Quieting the crowd, she said, "We'll move this into the cafeteria, people. A lot more space is there." With cheers, the double doors opened wide, and everybody streamed into the cafeteria, settling into various spots around the room.

Jessica walked alongside Lance as they headed to the cafeteria. "Where do you think you want to sit?"

"I'm not sure," he said, as he entered the room, surveying the situation. "Maybe somewhere in the middle here against that back wall." So that's what they did. They set him up a chair, and he grabbed his guitar and said, "Good evening, everyone. Glad you could all make it." And, with that, he headed into a several renditions of John Denver songs and then did a Barry White, which just caused her heart to swim with joy.

When he slid into several jazz songs, she hit Record on

her phone because, dear God, his music was unbelievable. She didn't want to lose that magic. When he was done at an hour and a half, she had tears in her eyes, and she could see several men in the room choking back their emotions as well. Somehow Lance had taken it to a whole new level tonight.

She didn't know how or why, but every soul in that room was affected. What Lance could do with that little guitar was nothing short of amazing. And, when he finally came to an end, there was dead silence, and then the place erupted in cheers.

He smiled, looking a little emotional himself. "That went a little deep tonight," he said. "I hope you guys are all okay with that. I tend to play by the moods that I'm in, and, tonight, well, it just seemed appropriate to play some of these songs."

Jessica got up, walked over to the cafeteria water table, and poured herself a glass, waiting for the emotions to slide back down her throat. Dani joined her.

"My God," Dani whispered. "He's so good."

"I know," Jessica said. "I can't believe it."

"Well, we'll see what comes of it tonight," Dani said with a tiny smile. Jessica looked at her suspiciously. Dani gave a shrug and said, "One never knows where one can be."

"I recorded some of that tonight," Jessica said. "I just wanted to have that music myself. But I should ask him if it's okay."

"Right. We never thought of that, did we? But we should be recording him, if only to preserve it for his own uses," Dani said, speaking more to herself now.

After dinner, Jessica and Lance sat outside together with a cup of tea.

"Lance, I recorded some of that tonight," she said. "I

never thought to ask you ahead of time. I just did it so I can have it and listen again, and I'd really like to keep it, but I'll understand if you'd rather I didn't."

"Play it, would you?" he said, looking at her in surprise.

She found the recording and played it, letting several songs drift across the open deck as the two of them sat out here alone.

"I missed a note on that one," he said.

"That's the only thing you can say?" she said, laughing. "Did you realize there wasn't a dry eye in the room?"

"Hey, I was feeling kind of teary-eyed myself," he said. "That's the problem with playing from the heart," he said. "Once your heart's engaged, it comes through, and it's hard not to be affected by the music."

"It was stunning," she said. "So," she said, when she stopped the recording, "can I keep it?"

He looked at her and said, "Do you really want to? I made a couple mistakes."

She chuckled. "Apparently I wouldn't know the difference," she said. "The music moved me to the point of tears, and I would just love to have it."

"Okay then," he said, "but you're not selling it or anything, right?"

"I won't be playing it for the managers at the two clubs in town. That's up to you to decide." She chuckled. "My personal use only."

"Fine," he said with a dismissive wave.

"But you could consider selling something like this," she said. "I know you don't want to do that YouTube thing, but I think there's a lot of room for somebody as talented as you are."

"Well, so says you," he said with a gentle smile. "The

thing about musicians is that it's really hard to stand out. There are just so many of us, and some are truly gifted," he said. "It's a sea of voices, and you're trying to be the one who gets heard," he said. "It doesn't really work too well for most."

"So you say," she said because, inside, she couldn't imagine anybody not clamoring to hear his music. Especially with the emotions he poured into it. "Tonight you were truly brilliant."

LANCE REMEMBERED JESSICA'S words over the next couple days, and they put a little spring in his step and a smile on his face.

Even Shane commented on it. "Man, you had the place in tears the other night," he said.

"Not sure that's a good thing, is it?" Lance said. "Considering most of them already have experienced some pretty difficult traumas in their lives."

"True," Shane said, "but everybody needs an outlet for their feelings too."

"I wasn't thinking of that," he said.

"Nope, we rarely do," he said. "Now that you're heading into your last couple months, from what I can see, how are you feeling about your progress?"

"Considering that I didn't really see any potential for much progress," he said, "I can't believe how strong and vibrant I feel now."

"Inside and out?"

"Inside and out," he said. "And honestly, I think the music is responsible for a lot of that inside."

"And once the inside fires up," Shane said, "it's like you can't do anything but keep the outside going too," he said. "Once you got music back into your life, your progress moved in leaps and bounds."

"It feels wonderful," he said. "I still haven't figured out what to do with my life, but you know what? I'm not sure that I have to do very much either."

"Good point," Shane said. "Too often everybody thinks they have to get a nine-to-five job, but I'm not sure that's true in your case, is it?"

Lance shook his head. "No, it isn't. I do have some income," he said. "It's not exactly enough to buy a house and to raise a family, but I might just take a few months and see about writing some of the songs that are in my soul," he confessed. "Since I've started feeling better," he said, "I've gotten back to writing."

"I didn't even know you wrote songs too," Shane said in surprise. "If you can pack as much emotion into those songs as you did into Saturday night's performance," he said, "they are bound to be a big hit."

"There might be a big hit among them," he said, "but in this world nobody can hear you because so many other great musicians are out there."

"Maybe," Shane said, "but there's also an awful lot of recording contracts for talented souls," he said. "I think that anytime somebody's really good, an avenue is out there for him to be heard."

"I could always give lessons," he said and then made a face. "But that really doesn't have much appeal at this point."

"How about just playing at weddings and stuff?"

"That doesn't appeal either," he said. "Maybe bars again

though." Then he mentioned the email that Jessica had brought him a couple weeks earlier, if not a month ago by now.

"That might be a great idea," Shane said. "If you can get by with working a couple nights a week, and that's enough to tide you over for now," he said, "why not? One of the things I'd like to see in your life is to avoid the heavy stress load that you used to have," he said. "Nothing sets someone back further than that kind of stress. I've seen it bring the healing to a complete stop."

"I hear you," Lance said, "and that was something I was just considering."

"You need to figure out what you'll do when you're done here," he said, "so you have a place to go. That's a part of the exit planning. It doesn't have to be a forever plan but should offer a solid transition that is good for several months at least."

"I know," he said. "I just haven't managed to get to town to figure out the housing element."

"Talk to Dani about it," he said. "Nobody here does the transition without her help," Shane said in a serious tone. "The fact that you're even looking at a transition is huge, and I'm not saying it'll be a month from now because I don't know where the rest of your team is at," he said. "But I am telling you that I hope to get you to that 100 percent by the end of the month."

"Except I'm looking for that one-twenty," he said.

Shane grinned. "That's all right," he said, "and, if you reach for that same 120 percent in your music," he said, "you'll go very far."

"I'm not even looking to go far," he said. "I think I'm looking to write the music of my heart and to maybe use that to heal the rest of me," he said.

"Go for it," Shane said. "I can't imagine anything better for you."

Chapter 16

TWO DAYS LATER, on Friday, Lance asked her a question that really surprised her.

"Where do you live?"

"I've been living at Hathaway House," she said, "though that won't be for much longer though."

"Why is that?" he asked, looking at her in surprise. "You're moving?"

"It was supposed to be temporary, just to get settled," she said, "and the temporary turned to all this time. I should be heading back into town, where I can carve out more of a life beyond Hathaway House, so I am vacating my apartment for another employee."

"Ouch," he said. "That sounds like you're trying to get away from me."

"Really? I wouldn't expect that you would be here all that much longer," she teased.

He nodded. "That's true, and I was figuring out about an apartment or something in town, since I won't be here forever."

"Right," she said. "Maybe a ground-floor place?"

"Maybe," he said, "or at least no stairs. I guess I could handle an elevator. I'd kind of like to be more in the country though," he said. "I just don't know what the options are."

"I don't either," she said, "but Dani would be a good

resource on that."

"Of course," he said with a laugh. "It sounds like Dani has the information on a ton of things."

"She doesn't get rid of people just because they're done at Hathaway," she said with a smile. "I know she visits some of the guys who used to live here. She checks up on them to make sure that they're adapting well to the outside world."

"Nice," he said. "It doesn't happen all that often to find a place like Hathaway House that is run by somebody with as much heart as Dani has."

"That's why she does what she does," Jessica said.

"Well, maybe she can help me find a place a couple months down the road."

"And those couple months will go by fast," Jessica said. "Too fast, really."

"Meaning?" he challenged.

She shrugged self-consciously. "Meaning, I'll miss you," she said.

He reached across and gripped her fingers. "I'm not going far," he said, "and you said you were planning to move into town yourself."

"Maybe," she said, looking around. "This has been a really good place for me, but sometimes I wonder if it isn't too easy to be complacent here," she said. "I don't get out and meet other people, and you know I used to love going to the blues club," she said. "However, living out here, I tend not to go anywhere because I have to go into town to do it."

"But, on the other hand, how will you feel driving out here to work every day?" he asked.

"I'm not sure about that either," she said. "If I got something on this side of Dallas, where I don't have to deal with the traffic, it would be a quick hop to work every day. Then

I'm already three-quarters of the way there, if I wanted to go do something in town, so it's not nearly as stressful."

"Stress is the big progress killer," he said. "That's what Shane told me that I'm supposed to avoid."

"Good luck with that," she said. "It's something we all have to deal with."

"It is, indeed," he said. "I'll talk to Dani first and see if she has any ideas."

"Do that," she said. "Have you worked up your songs for tomorrow night?"

"Yes," he said. "I was hoping to play just a few, to keep to Dani's schedule, but that won't work. I can't wait until tomorrow."

BY THE TIME he got there at four p.m. that Saturday, the songs thrummed through his body, and he couldn't wait for his fingers to touch the guitar strings and the piano keys. He started off in the same community room, not sure if it would be the same size crowd again. He didn't have the piano in the cafeteria. It was on wheels, but he didn't know that anybody was prepared to move it. However, as he sat down at his place with his guitar, he frowned because the piano wasn't here.

Dani walked by, smiled, crooked her finger at him, and said, "We're in the other room."

"It got bigger, did it?" he asked, with a sheepish grin.

"Way bigger," she said, a mysteriously secretive air to her. She looked particularly smug.

He pondered that for a moment, then stepped into the cafeteria to see that easily one hundred people were here, all waiting for him. As soon as he arrived, they all clapped and cheered. He shrugged self-consciously, but he walked up on his crutches to his designated chair and sat down. As soon as he started to play, the crowd calmed down. He lost himself immediately in the music, starting with an Aretha Franklin song which flowed into another then another.

As the music flowed from his fingers, Lance also sang along. He would often sing when he did his music before, but he hadn't done that since he had started playing again. He didn't realize it now, until he opened his eyes at the end of the song to see everybody staring at him in amazement. He shrugged and said, "Well, I guess you never know what to expect here, right?"

There was a lot of laughter and clapping. Lance hopped up, grabbed his crutches, walked to the piano, and started ripping into some rock and roll. Before long, the whole dining area was filled with people stomping and clapping in time. Lance went through several of his favorites, and, when he finally came to a crashing crescendo at the end, and then stopped, he had timed it perfectly to be done an hour and a half later. He waited for the silence to fall, and then the entire room erupted in cheers. Just as he turned around, arms came around him, and he was hugged from behind. He twisted and wrapped his arms around Jessica. "I figured it was you," he murmured.

She leaned over and kissed him on the cheek. "How could it not be?" she said. "That was absolutely amazing."

With a smile he realized that Dennis had come over with some drinks on trays, handing them out to everybody. When the tray was offered to him, Lance said to Dennis, "You never miss a trick to show what a good guy you are, do you?"

Dennis laughed with a pleased smile. "Tonight deserves

something special," he said. "You really outdid yourself. Do you have any idea how good this is for all these guys and gals?"

"I feel great," he said.

Shane stood off to the side, nodding. "I heard that," he said. "And that deserves a drink." Everybody raised their glasses in a toast to Lance.

He smiled, raised his, and took a sip. It was hot chocolate, warm with a hint of cinnamon, and it was great. They sat down, as he just relaxed. He noticed a couple people he'd never seen before in the background. When he looked again, they were gone, but then he saw them near the door, talking to Dani. He raised an eyebrow at Dani, and she just shrugged. Of course she knew a ton more people than Lance did. Heck, he was still trying to figure out who was a patient and who was staff in this place sometimes.

But he headed off to bed that night with a smile, and his future had never looked brighter. A couple days later he got an email from the blues club in town. He stared at it because he hadn't realized what the name of the place was, but it was well-renowned, and people flew in from all over the country to spend time there. As he read the email, his jaw dropped. He was being asked to come and do a debut session on the Friday night, two weeks hence. He just shook his head and stared.

What an honor, he thought, but how would they even have known about him? Surely that's not the bar that Jessica had been to, was it? He racked his brain, wondering if she had mentioned the bar's name. Because this one was bigger than big. He hadn't even realized it was here in Dallas, mistakenly thinking it was in Austin. As he did the research on it, he realized that every blues singer that he had ever held in high regard had played there.

Of course he liked to play all kinds of music, but this place offered the blues. And they were specifically asking him to come, not to audition, but to sit in and play for an hour and a half. He sank back on the bed and stared at the ceiling, dumbfounded. When Shane walked in, Lance looked up and said, "Problems?"

"I was going to ask you that," he said. "It's Tuesday, and you were due at my session ten minutes ago."

Lance looked at him in shock. "What time is it?"

"Almost nine-fifteen," Shane said. "And you're still in bed. What gives?"

"I have no idea," he said. "I went to bed exhausted, and I guess I must have slept in," he said. "I haven't even had breakfast."

"Well, you aren't getting any now," he said. "I want to make sure those shoulders and arms of yours are loosened up."

"Right," he said. "Well, give me two minutes to get dressed, and I'll get down to the gym." He twisted the laptop around and pointed to the email and said, "While I'm getting dressed, see what you make of that." As he went to the washroom and quickly changed, he came out, then went back in. "I don't know if this is a good thing or a bad thing," he said, "but I came out without the crutches and had to go back and get them."

Shane looked at him with a smile on his face. "It's a hugely good thing," he said. "You'll do a lot more walking without them from now on." He tapped the laptop and said, "What are we talking about crutches for? This is freaking amazing. What an opportunity!"

"I knew that Dallas had blues clubs," he said, "but I

didn't realize *this* one was here. Holy cow."

"Dallas's well known for its jazz and also the blues," he said with a smile. "This club is world-renowned for their blues."

"I know," he said. "I don't have a clue how they knew about me, unless it's the one that Jessica went to a few months ago. She just said, *the blues club*, and I got a case of cold feet, so we never really talked about it again."

"That's because, even though there are others in town, it's really *the* blues club," Shane said.

Just the thought of being invited kept a smile on his face throughout Shane's hard workout. Then when he discovered he'd lost his wheelchair on a permanent basis, he turned cranky.

"Deal with it," Shane said. "It's holding you back at this point. Let the crutches be your crutch instead."

"But sometimes, when I'm tired," he said, "the wheelchair makes life so much easier."

"That's the thing about a crutch," he said, "and you just can't afford that right now."

"And I need to do things in my own time frame," he snapped back. When he hit the cafeteria for lunch, he was really hungry and could have been considered "hangry." Hungry plus angry. He loaded up with protein and veggies and sat down on his own off to the side, digging into his food.

When Dennis arrived with a cup of coffee a little bit later, he said, "Man, you're hungry today."

"I missed breakfast," he mumbled. "And Shane put me to work. Then we had an argument." He sat back with a heavy sigh and said, "But I do feel better now."

"Never argue on an empty stomach," Dennis said. "It's a

well-known fact that hungry people don't make a whole lot of sense sometimes."

"Well, I was definitely hungry," he said. "Now that I've eaten so fast, I don't think I can finish this."

"Give it a few minutes," Dennis said. "You'll probably find out you've got room for it after all."

Laughing at that, he said, "Okay, I'll give it a shot, and thanks for the coffee."

"Not a problem," Dennis said and moved on.

Lance realized that he really had been cranky mostly because of the wheelchair thing. He'd come down with his crutches, and, as he stood to return his dirty dishes, he realized he was walking without the crutches too. He slowly made his way back to the table, grabbed his crutches, and used them to get back to his bedroom. It was also his shrink day. Using his crutches, he headed down to the office, and, when he knocked, he was invited in right away.

The doctor took one look at him on the crutches and said, "Progress, indeed."

"Progress on many levels," he said and explained about the email.

"So, will you do it?"

"I'm not sure," he said.

The doctor just stared at him, then slowly leaned forward. "You want to explain?"

"Because I'm not sure I'm ready," he said. "Although I'm better, I don't want to have some stupid deal where I fall off the stage or where I can't sit on the chair and my back seizes up, or you know? It wasn't so bad, but then Shane chose today to take away my wheelchair permanently," he confessed.

The doctor, a small smile playing at the corner of his

mouth, sat back. "Ah, so you lost something that was part of yourself. Something that made you feel secure, so now everything else in the future looks scary, doesn't it?"

He frowned at the shrink. "Surely it can't be that simple, can it?"

"Life is often that simple," he said. "And it makes sense, if you think about it. You were just getting really comfortable, but you also knew you had the wheelchair to fall back on."

"I can go buy my own wheelchair," he said, staring out the window.

"You can," he said, "and maybe that's what you need to do. Buy it and just keep it there as a reminder that, when things get bad, you can sit down and use it."

"Most people don't like their wheelchair," he said. "So what's wrong with me?"

"Nothing," he said, "but change is threatening for you. It always has been. So, if you need to hang on to that wheelchair a little bit longer, than you hang on to it."

He nodded slowly. "Not sure Shane will let me."

"I'll have a talk with Shane," the doc said. "If you want it, you can have it. Just let me know."

Chapter 17

SOMETHING WAS GOING on that Jessica wasn't too sure about. Lance seemed excited and ready to tell her something and then had backed off several times. She went up to Dani on Thursday and asked, "Do you know what's going on with Lance?"

Dani looked up at her, surprised. "What do you mean by *going on*?"

She frowned and said, "He seems really excited about something, yet he won't tell me what it is."

"Maybe you'll have to wait for him to share it then," she said.

"I hate waiting," she said, "and, during all the time that I'm waiting, it always seems like I'm looking at the negative side of life instead of the positive."

"So then patience in this instance is a good thing," Dani said gently. "And you can do whatever you want to do, but it's up to him to tell you when he's ready."

Jessica started to nod and then looked at her and asked, "Do you know?"

Dani grinned. "I know something's going on. I don't know what it is you're talking about in particular though."

With that, Jessica had to be satisfied, and she headed off.

As she headed down the hallway, Shane called out to her, "I'm going into town and maybe to the blues club just to get away for a bit. Do you want to come? I think a group of us are going," he said.

"You know what? That would be nice," she said. "Music tonight and then potentially again tomorrow night with Lance."

"We'll miss him when he's gone," Shane said. "A couple more weeks and he's likely to have his strings cut."

"He's sure come a long way, and that's what we want for everybody," she said warmly. But, in her heart of hearts, she also knew that she would be lonely as heck without him. And that's not what she wanted. But she was willing to do whatever she needed to do in order to help him fly. "So what time are you going?"

"Well, it'll start around seven-thirty, I think," he said. "So we should be there by six-thirty or seven to be sure we get seats."

"Good enough," she said.

"We'll take the van after dinner."

"Okay, that sounds good. Thank you for asking me."

As it was, baked sea bass was served for dinner, so she thoroughly enjoyed her meal, and then she found a group of about eight of them gathered and ready to go. They got into one of the big Hathaway vans and headed into town.

"We don't usually get this many people to go," she said.

He looked at her, smiled, and said, "No, we don't. But that's all right. Sometimes we have special events for everybody." The drive into town went by quickly, and, in another five minutes, they were at the blues club. As they drove in to the parking lot, she was amazed.

"Just think, it's only a quarter to seven, and the place is packed." Then she cried out, "Oh, look. Another group from Hathaway House is here."

"Yeah, I heard that," Shane said, then hopped out, opened the panel door, and everybody climbed out.

"Now we have to get seats," she said.

He nodded. "Hopefully it won't be that bad." As they walked into the dusky atmosphere, already some music was playing up front. He grabbed her arm and pointed to a bunch of tables roped off in the back. "It's full enough now that we might go in there." Another Hathaway House employee was back there too, so they all sat down together.

Jessica smiled. "Gosh, it's too bad Lance isn't here," she said. "This would be perfect for him to see how this place works and all."

"Yeah," Shane said, as waitresses came around, and they all ordered drinks. As she sat here talking to another nurse, one of the announcers stepped onto the stage.

"Have we got a treat for you tonight, guys. He's new to our blues club, but he certainly isn't new to the blues scene. We knew his name many, many years ago, but we never had a chance to bring him in. His life took several turns—some up, some down, and, in his case, the last few years have been pretty rough. But he's on the road to recovery now, and I want you to welcome Lance Mayfair for the next hour and a half. He'll be a treat for your ears and a sight for sore eyes."

Just then, the light shone on the man sitting in the center of the stage, his fingers immediately picking at the strings of the guitar and pouring out music the likes of which she had never heard before. Her jaw dropped, and she looked over at Shane and caught sight of his big grin. "You knew?"

He nodded. "He got the invite a couple weeks ago. He was going to come alone and was trying to arrange with Dani a way to get here. We decided that, if we support them at Hathaway House, we'll support them in town too. And, once we got word out that he was coming to play, we all wanted to come and see him. Look around," he said, as he pointed out about two dozen other Hathaway residents, thoroughly enjoying the outing.

But her gaze was stuck on Lance. With his head back and his throat full, he sang songs that she'd never heard come from him before. When he substituted a trumpet for the guitar and lit into another blues number, everybody crying and cheering, she had tears streaming down her face. "Oh, my God," she said. "He is so incredibly talented."

"He is," Shane said. "And, up until now, I think he was just a broken soul. He'd walked away from all this to serve his country, and now he's at a whole new place in his life where this can be his new world."

And to see him up there without his wheelchair, only then to realize she saw no crutches … "How did he get on the stage?" she marveled.

Shane reached across, tapped her hand gently, and whispered, "He walked. Just like he's been walking everywhere recently. Haven't you seen him?"

She nodded, yet frowned. "Sure, but it's been so crazy again lately that I've been late coming to see him at lunch or just stopping in his room, so I haven't really seen him walking on his own," she whispered. "That is incredible." As she looked over at the other Hathaway House people, she saw Dani sitting there with Dennis, who caught her gaze, and he lifted his drink.

"Oh, my God, even Dennis is here."

"Are you kidding?" Shane said. "Everybody wanted to come, but we only had so many vans." And she knew why. Because, when this man makes music, he makes everybody's heart sing. And she sat back to watch the rest of the evening.

When it finally came to an end, there wasn't a dry eye in the place. As his fingers slowed, and the music drifted over their heads on the last refrain, the place erupted as everybody stood to cheer. She knew that, of all the things he planned on doing, this was his return to the world, and she had just watched him making his first mark as a smashing success.

LANCE LISTENED TO the applause, feeling his heart settle and his soul relax. He realized that this was the thing he'd always wanted to do in the back of his mind. God and country came first, and then his music. And now it was time. When everybody stood, stomping and cheering for an encore, he lifted a hand, and immediately there was silence. He said, "I do have one more song. It's not exactly a blues song," he said, "but I'd like to sing it and to dedicate it to one person who's been a guiding light at my side for the last many months, as I've made the journey from being a fully broken-down man to the partly broken-down man you see before you now. She's been there giving me confidence, pushing me when I didn't want to be pushed, and walking away when I needed to be left alone. She is here in the audience tonight," he said, "so this song is for her."

And he started singing "Sweet Caroline." And the audience loved it.

Everybody turned to see where Jessica sat. Beside Shane, she smiled with tears in her eyes, the tears slowly dripping down her cheeks, as Lance said that the song was just for her.

When it was over and done, there was a moment of silence, and then Lance whispered through the mic, "You'll always be in my heart, honey. And I hope one day to make you mine."

The place erupted as she burst from her chair, raced to the stage, and was beside him in two seconds flat to wrap her arms around him. As soon as he saw her coming, he stood, opened his arms, and held her close.

She was bawling in his arms, but he knew that they were happy tears, and he just held her close.

"I didn't tell you," he whispered against her hair, "because I wanted to surprise you. I've always been the one hanging back, the one taking his own sweet time, while you were out there pumping and jumping, ready to go. I wanted to show you that this time I was ready too." And he tilted up her chin, looked down, and kissed her. And even he couldn't hear the sounds of the noise around them. He only heard her words.

"I love you so much," Jessica whispered to him.

He wrapped his arms around her and held her close.

More than ready for the future standing in front of him.

Epilogue

AT TIMES IN Melissa's life, she'd made rash decisions. Most of them had turned out okay. Sometimes not. Then sometimes she deliberated for so long that the opportunities passed her by.

She stared down at the crumpled letter in her lap. Not just crumpled but also tearstained. Her one and only friend had gone to the trouble to track her down, even after years of silence. Then Dani had known Melissa before her parents' death. Afterward she'd moved into Dani's place as a retreat. They'd finished school together. Then Melissa had entered the navy and what she had hoped would be a brand-new life.

And it had been, … until her accident.

Now she was at a crossroads yet again. And this time, once more, Dani offered a pathway open to Melissa. Back then Dani had pleaded with Melissa to continue staying with her and her father and to not go into service. She'd chosen the navy over her friend back then.

Now Melissa had a chance to choose Dani this time. She had spent many years building up a VA rehab center called Hathaway House—originally built to help her father regain a life after his own injuries had sidelined his military career. With the upstairs part of this center growing, Dani had quickly installed a veterinarian clinic down below. Then that was Dani; she couldn't help herself from trying to save the world, one person, one animal at a time.

Just as she had tried to save Melissa back then, Dani was trying to save Melissa now.

She had refused back then, but now …

Looking around her four-person room, Melissa took in the apparatus attached to her bed, the wheelchair, and the crutches close by. The life she lived here, while recovering from her latest surgery, was filled with hopelessness at the thought of staying here. In reflection, going into the navy had felt like she was running away instead of running to a new future.

Now it felt the same again.

On impulse she picked up her phone and called Dani. When Melissa heard her friend's voice, her throat closed.

"Hello? Hello?"

"Dani," she finally got out.

Silence. Then Dani exploded, "Melissa?"

"Yeah," she said, half in tears, half in laughter.

"Oh my, I'm so glad you called. I'd be even happier if you've filled out that application to come here.'

"No, I haven't. At least not yet."

"Please do it," Dani pleaded. "We can help you here."

"I don't know if you can," she whispered back. "I'm in pain all the time. The journey itself will be incredibly hard."

"Yes, it could be," Dani said quietly. "But, once here, we have specialists on staff who can help you."

Melissa sniffled her tears back. She wanted to believe her friend. She really did. But hope was a little thin on the ground.

"Please," Dani said into the phone. "Take a leap of faith. Let me help. Last time I pleaded with you to stay. This time I'm asking you to come. You needed someone back then and walked away. You need someone now. Please don't walk away from me this time."

Melissa took a deep breath and capitulated. "All right. I just hope you know what you're doing."

"I do," Dani said. "Come. You won't regret it."

This concludes Book 12 of Hathaway House: Lance.

Read about Melissa: Hathaway House, Book 13

Hathaway House: Melissa (Book #13)

***Welcome to Hathaway House. Rehab Center. Safe Haven.
Second chance at life and love.***

Health-care worker Shane has been at Hathaway House since
the beginning. He's watched patient after patient scratch and
claw their way to recovery and has watched relationship after
relationship blossom into love and marriage. He believes in
love. Wants a true love of his own. Yet he wonders now
whether anyone is out there for him.

Until Melissa walks into his gym.

Broken and beaten by life and overwhelmed with endless
pain was never part of Melissa's long-term plan. But a year
after an accident sidelined her navy career, she's still fighting
her way back to a normal life—if such a thing exists for the
woman she's become. Her transfer to Hathaway House is a
lifeline to her oldest friend, but, even with Dani's encour-
agement, Melissa's journey back to health is long and hard
and maybe just a pipe dream. But she'll try again. One more
time.

Separately, Shane and Melissa have been battling their own personal demons. When they meet at Hathaway House, the tough physiotherapist vows that his newest client will reach successes unimaginable to her. Together, working through her rehab plan, Shane and Melissa find a special tenderness behind each other's strength.

Find Book 13 here!

To find out more visit Dale Mayer's website.

http://smarturl.it/DMSMelissa

Author's Note

Thank you for reading Lance: Hathaway House, Book 12! If you enjoyed the book, please take a moment and leave a short review.

Dear reader,

I love to hear from readers, and you can contact me at my website: www.dalemayer.com or at my Facebook author page. To be informed of new releases and special offers, sign up for my newsletter or follow me on BookBub. And if you are interested in joining Dale Mayer's Reader Group, here is the Facebook sign up page.
https://smarturl.it/DaleMayerFBGroup

Cheers,
Dale Mayer

Get THREE Free Books Now!

Have you met the SEALS of Honor?

SEALs of Honor Books 1, 2, and 3. Follow the stories of brave, badass warriors who serve their country with honor and love their women to the limits of life and death.

Read Mason, Hawk, and Dane right now for FREE.

Go here and tell me where to send them!
http://smarturl.it/EthanBofB

About the Author

Dale Mayer is a USA Today bestselling author best known for her Psychic Visions and Family Blood Ties series. Her contemporary romances are raw and full of passion and emotion (Second Chances, SKIN), her thrillers will keep you guessing (By Death series), and her romantic comedies will keep you giggling (It's a Dog's Life and Charmin Marvin Romantic Comedy series).

She honors the stories that come to her – and some of them are crazy and break all the rules and cross multiple genres!

To go with her fiction, she also writes nonfiction in many different fields with books available on resume writing, companion gardening and the US mortgage system. She has recently published her Career Essentials Series. All her books are available in print and ebook format.

Connect with Dale Mayer Online

Dale's Website – www.dalemayer.com
Facebook Personal – https://smarturl.it/DaleMayerFacebook
Instagram – https://smarturl.it/DaleMayerInstagram
BookBub – https://smarturl.it/DaleMayerBookbub
Facebook Fan Page – https://smarturl.it/DaleMayerFBFanPage
Goodreads – https://smarturl.it/DaleMayerGoodreads

Also by Dale Mayer

Published Adult Books:

Hathaway House
Aaron, Book 1
Brock, Book 2
Cole, Book 3
Denton, Book 4
Elliot, Book 5
Finn, Book 6
Gregory, Book 7
Heath, Book 8
Iain, Book 9
Jaden, Book 10
Keith, Book 11
Lance, Book 12
Melissa, Book 13

The K9 Files
Ethan, Book 1
Pierce, Book 2
Zane, Book 3
Blaze, Book 4
Lucas, Book 5
Parker, Book 6
Carter, Book 7
Weston, Book 8
Greyson, Book 9

Ice Maiden
Psychic Visions Books 1–3
Psychic Visions Books 4–6
Psychic Visions Books 7–9

By Death Series
Touched by Death
Haunted by Death
Chilled by Death
By Death Books 1–3

Broken Protocols – Romantic Comedy Series
Cat's Meow
Cat's Pajamas
Cat's Cradle
Cat's Claus
Broken Protocols 1-4

Broken and... Mending
Skin
Scars
Scales (of Justice)
Broken but… Mending 1-3

Glory
Genesis
Tori
Celeste
Glory Trilogy

Biker Blues
Morgan: Biker Blues, Volume 1
Cash: Biker Blues, Volume 2

SEALs of Honor

Heroes for Hire

Levi's Legend: Heroes for Hire, Book 1
Stone's Surrender: Heroes for Hire, Book 2
Merk's Mistake: Heroes for Hire, Book 3
Rhodes's Reward: Heroes for Hire, Book 4
Flynn's Firecracker: Heroes for Hire, Book 5
Logan's Light: Heroes for Hire, Book 6
Harrison's Heart: Heroes for Hire, Book 7
Saul's Sweetheart: Heroes for Hire, Book 8
Dakota's Delight: Heroes for Hire, Book 9
Michael's Mercy (Part of Sleeper SEAL Series)
Tyson's Treasure: Heroes for Hire, Book 10
Jace's Jewel: Heroes for Hire, Book 11
Rory's Rose: Heroes for Hire, Book 12
Brandon's Bliss: Heroes for Hire, Book 13
Liam's Lily: Heroes for Hire, Book 14
North's Nikki: Heroes for Hire, Book 15
Anders's Angel: Heroes for Hire, Book 16
Reyes's Raina: Heroes for Hire, Book 17
Dezi's Diamond: Heroes for Hire, Book 18
Vince's Vixen: Heroes for Hire, Book 19
Ice's Icing: Heroes for Hire, Book 20
Johan's Joy: Heroes for Hire, Book 21
Galen's Gemma: Heroes for Hire, Book 22
Heroes for Hire, Books 1–3
Heroes for Hire, Books 4–6
Heroes for Hire, Books 7–9
Heroes for Hire, Books 10–12
Heroes for Hire, Books 13–15

SEALs of Steel

Badger: SEALs of Steel, Book 1

Erick: SEALs of Steel, Book 2
Cade: SEALs of Steel, Book 3
Talon: SEALs of Steel, Book 4
Laszlo: SEALs of Steel, Book 5
Geir: SEALs of Steel, Book 6
Jager: SEALs of Steel, Book 7
The Final Reveal: SEALs of Steel, Book 8
SEALs of Steel, Books 1–4
SEALs of Steel, Books 5–8
SEALs of Steel, Books 1–8

The Mavericks
Kerrick, Book 1
Griffin, Book 2
Jax, Book 3
Beau, Book 4
Asher, Book 5
Ryker, Book 6
Miles, Book 7
Nico, Book 8
Keane, Book 9
Lennox, Book 10
Gavin, Book 11
Shane, Book 12

Bullard's Battle Series
Ryland's Reach, Book 1
Cain's Cross, Book 2
Eton's Escape, Book 3
Garret's Gambit, Book 4
Kano's Keep, Book 5
Fallon's Flaw, Book 6
Quinn's Quest, Book 7

Bullard's Beauty, Book 8

Collections
Dare to Be You…
Dare to Love…
Dare to be Strong…
RomanceX3

Standalone Novellas
It's a Dog's Life
Riana's Revenge
Second Chances

Published Young Adult Books:

Family Blood Ties Series
Vampire in Denial
Vampire in Distress
Vampire in Design
Vampire in Deceit
Vampire in Defiance
Vampire in Conflict
Vampire in Chaos
Vampire in Crisis
Vampire in Control
Vampire in Charge
Family Blood Ties Set 1–3
Family Blood Ties Set 1–5
Family Blood Ties Set 4–6
Family Blood Ties Set 7–9
Sian's Solution, A Family Blood Ties Series Prequel
    Novelette

Design series
Dangerous Designs
Deadly Designs
Darkest Designs
Design Series Trilogy

Standalone
In Cassie's Corner
Gem Stone (a Gemma Stone Mystery)
Time Thieves

Published Non-Fiction Books:

Career Essentials
Career Essentials: The Résumé
Career Essentials: The Cover Letter
Career Essentials: The Interview
Career Essentials: 3 in 1

Printed in Great Britain
by Amazon